John Stark is a man with one purpose in life: to destroy the Company. Any way he can, regardless of who gets in his way.
The Company is an international crime syndicate dealing in every kind of activity that will make money out of human degradation. It has killed everyone Stark holds dear and he is out to take his own kind of bloody vengeance on the murderers concerned. His path of revenge leads him from a prison break in England to the capital cities of the world, and behind him he leaves a trail of Company corpses. Stark is a hunter – hunted himself by his victims and the law alike.

John Stark is the Revenger.

Also by Joseph Hedges and available from Sphere Books

THE REVENGER: FUNERAL RITES
THE REVENGER: THE CHINESE COFFIN

The Revenger: Arms for Oblivion

JOSEPH HEDGES

SPHERE BOOKS LIMITED
30/32 Gray's Inn Road, London WCIX 8JL

First published in Great Britain
by Sphere Books Ltd 1973

Reprinted 1974

TRADE
MARK

Set in Linotype Baskerville

Printed in Great Britain by
Hazell Watson & Viney Ltd
Aylesbury, Bucks

ISBN 0 7221 4312 5

THE REVENGER:
ARMS FOR OBLIVION

CHAPTER ONE

As the Boeing seven-two-seven of Alitalia drifted down through the shimmering heat haze, rays of Mediterranean sunlight struck glancing blows at its ports. The landing wheels screeched on the runway and printed black rubber marks against the grey concrete. There was no bounce: just the inevitable thunder of the three turbofan engines as they were kicked into reverse thrust and the thumping judder as the airliner lost speed.

The pretty stewardess reminded the passengers not to leave any personal belongings in the cabin and warned against smoking until they were transferred to the terminal building. She made the initial announcement in Italian and then followed up with translations in French and English. On behalf of the captain and crew she hoped her charges would have an enjoyable stay on the Côte d'Azur and would travel Alitalia in the future.

Sitting in the first-class section, Ralph Hooker did not listen to the announcement. Not by nature a nervous man nor, under normal circumstances, one with a religious bent, Hooker had an unreasoning dread of flying. So before each take-off he said a short prayer of hope and after landing he gave thanks. In between, he sweated a great deal.

But the stewardess had the full attention of the man seated beside Hooker, for Enrico Primo considered himself a connoisseur of women. And he invariably put boring in-flight time to good use by fantasising about the most beautiful woman on the aircraft. In his estimation this was almost always the air hostess and he was at a loss to understand the reason for this – until he flew from Rome to Munich on an occasion when he was seated next to a not very attractive British Wren captain. His mind had undergone paroxysms of wild imaginings and he was forced to conclude that his metabolism underwent some basic change whenever he entered an aircraft – turning him into a uniform fetishist. And it was only in the pressurised environment that it happened because on the ground he was much more discerning. For neither his wife in Milan, nor his two mistresses – one in the same city and another in Rome – had ever worn uniforms to his knowledge and he never felt the urge to see them thus attired.

Having accepted this strange trait in his character, Primo indulged it to his heart's content. So it was that, as Hooker silently gave thanks to heaven for his deliverance, the Italian beside him secretly read a sexual *double entendre* into every mundane phrase spoken by the girl with a mole on her neck and dimple on her chin.

Not until the Boeing had swung on to its parking area and the engines had whined to their rest did both men open their eyes and return to reality. Warm, unfiltered air tainted by jet fuel exhaust fumes rushed into the cabin as the hatchways were opened and passengers hustled to get off the aircraft.

'Good landing, Rico,' Hooker said with a smile as he released his seat belt.

'Didn't notice, I was thinking,' Primo replied, his English good with the nasal twang of an American accent.

Neither man was in any hurry as he retrieved his briefcase from beneath the seat and allowed the other first-class travellers to disembark ahead of him. The hostess who had occupied Primo's thoughts for the entire flight was standing at the head of the Alitalia stairway. Hooker thanked her politely; Primo negligently. The uniform meant nothing to him now and he found the mole a blemish marring her attractiveness.

Hooker began to sweat again as he crossed the apron in front of the terminal building, but this time from the heat rather than nervousness. For he was dressed in an impeccably cut suit of blue serge, with a white shirt, black tie, black patent shoes and a bowler hat. The only item missing from this typically British business garb was a rolled umbrella – he had managed to overcome Judith's insistence that he should take one by allowing her to pack a plastic mackintosh in his suitcase.

Primo was less uncomfortable in the humid heat, appropriately dressed in lightweight cream trousers, a blue jacket, multi-coloured open-necked shirt and sandals.

The fellow travellers were dissimilar in many other respects, too. Hooker was tall and slimly built, with a long, gaunt face set with grey eyes which gave nothing away. He had looked his actual age of fifty during the nerve-rending flight, when the flesh of his face had shown a network of tiny lines. But now, as he strolled into the shadows of the arrivals section of the airport terminal, he was relaxed and seemed to drop ten years.

Primo was short and stocky, with a very round face tanned to a light oak colour. He was five years younger than the Briton and almost bald but did not disguise the fact – as did Hooker – by wearing a hairpiece. But he did compensate for it by cultivating a bushy black moustache and growing his sideburns in widening curves towards his jaw. He had easy-smiling black eyes and an over-wide mouth that was at odds with his other features but somehow gave his face a sexual attractiveness it would not otherwise have had.

But the men did have at least two things in common. Both were top executives of Drake Enterprises Limited, a multi-national organisation with interests in oil-drilling and mineral mining, its shares quoted on every major stock exchange in the world. And both controlled policy decisions taken in respect of the companies operating in their native countries behind the cover of Drake Enterprises. Which meant that both Ralph Hooker and Enrico Primo had dirty fingers in the lucrative pies of narcotics, gambling, vice, gun-running, protection, extortion and many other illegal activities where high profit margins and careful planning off-set the risk element. As a spin-off from this, it also meant that both were directly or indirectly responsible for an incalculable amount of human suffering and widespread death.

Yet, as they strolled through passport control into the main concourse of Nice Airport, there was nothing about them to suggest that they were anything but a couple of respectable businessmen on their way to make a deal: and perhaps to mix a little pleasure with the business. This was precisely the impression top men of Drake Enterprises were supposed to create and their initial recruitment and ultimate promotion depended to a large extent upon their ability to do just this.

'Shall I do it, Ralph?' Primo asked as they crossed towards a bank of telephones on the wall.

Hooker nodded absently as he completed one searching

sweep of the concourse and began another, his eyes looking like blank pebbles under the lowered lids. Now, anyone with more than a passing curiosity about the two men might have been able to recognise a blemish in Hooker's veneer of respectability. For in his slightly tense stance and the impassive set of his gaunt features there was a trace of the furtive – a clue that he had something to hide or, perhaps, something to fear.

On the other hand, Primo was completely at ease as he fished a *jeton* from his jacket pocket, pushed it into the slot and lifted the receiver before dialling a number he knew by heart. But then Primo didn't have anybody like Stark to worry about.

'Hello, Hotel Concorde,' a woman answered.

'M. Flaud,' Primo requested.

As he waited for the room connection to be made, he glanced towards Hooker and caught a glimpse of the frown in profile. He guessed the reason for the Briton's anxiety, despite the fact that Hooker had not mentioned Stark either in Milan or during the flight.

'Flaud,' a man whispered hoarsely, as if he had a bad throat.

'The Milan flight just landed,' Primo said, giving a thumbs-up sign to Hooker as the latter looked in his direction. Primo's French was as good as his English. 'Any message?'

'There is one at the Air France desk,' Flaud confirmed. 'The name is Smith. Better ask your friend to get it.'

'Very bloody original,' Primo said wryly as the connection was broken and he replaced his own receiver.

Sure as he could be that they were not being watched, Hooker reverted to his placid demeanour as he listened to Primo. Then the two men moved over to the designated pick-up point and Hooker put his own French to the test in claiming to be named Smith and asking if there was a letter for him. There was: a sealed foolscap envelope which he ripped open with a long finger to reveal a single car ignition key in a folded sheet of paper. The short message was typewritten in unpunctuated English:

Audi NSU Ro8O bronze in short term car park meeting at three pm at place already arranged.

Hooker gave the note and key to Primo and then led the way out of the building, carefully placing the envelope in a litter basket. He had forgotten how hot it had been on the walk from the aircraft to the terminal and was unpleasantly surprised as the full glare of the afternoon sun hit him again. But now the air was scented with the perfume of the sub-tropical plants and flowers growing luxuriantly around the airport complex and he took a few moments to savour their sweet smells. His one regret about living in England was that he could only cultivate such plants in the carefully regulated atmosphere of his greenhouse at Cottonwood.

Then he set aside his discomfort in the heat and indulgence in his love for beautiful flowers to rake his impassive eyes over the cars and pedestrians milling along the pavements and roadways fronting the departure and arrival doors.

Primo noted this further sign of Hooker's preoccupation with his surroundings, but did not wish to broach the subject of Stark directly.

'If there was anything to worry about this end, Flaud would have given us the word,' he said.

Hooker was irritated that Primo had noticed his surreptitious surveillance of the bustling crowds. 'No harm in checking for oneself,' he said curtly.

Primo shrugged, nodded to a tall, model-slim girl with a poodle on a lead and drew a contemptuous stare in response. Then he led the way towards the car park, purposely setting a fast pace so that the sweating Hooker, weighed down by his suitcase, had to struggle to keep up.

The car that had been left for them was easy to find, parked close to the exit barrier.

It was unlocked and the driver's window was rolled down to its fullest extent. So the air inside was not stale – just hot. They tossed their cases on to the back seat and Primo shrugged out of his jacket and unbuttoned his shirt to the waist before sliding behind the wheel. Hooker did not even loosen his tie as he sat in the front passenger seat. But he took off the bowler and rested it on his lap.

Primo had never much cared for Hooker. He disliked the man's superior manner and constant striving for perfection in all things – no matter how unimportant. Primo considered he loved his own wife and four children as much as Hooker worshipped his family, but resented the Briton's indignation whenever the subject of his mistresses was raised. And he was jealous of the efficiency with which Hooker ran the United Kingdom end of the company's business – which tended to show in a bad light the operations in other countries, Italy among them.

But the renegade Stark had thrown a very large spanner indeed into the smooth-working machinery of the United Kingdom operation so that the calm complacency of Ralph Hooker had suffered a severe blow.* Primo had been ready to enjoy Hooker's discomfiture in Milan but the tall, gaunt-faced man had been able to successfully create an impression that nothing was wrong.

Now the strain had become too great and his guard was slipping. This was something to which Primo had been looking forward – the high and mighty Ralph Hooker losing his cool.

The car was new to Primo and he spent several moments familiarising himself with the facia instruments and controls. He sensed Hooker's mounting impatience and prolonged the exercise.

'Can't Italians drive anything but a Fiat?' the Briton snapped at length.

In the company hierarchy both men shared equal status, with Hooker carrying a little more weight at international board meetings because of his better profit record. But they were not at a board meeting now, and after the havoc Stark had caused, Primo doubted whether Hooker would ever again be allowed to steamroller his own views over the wishes of others.

Primo grinned at the sweating Hooker. 'Sure, Ralph,' he answered. 'I just bought myself a Lancia Flavia Coupé. I reckon it could outrun this buggy.'

Hooker was aware of Primo's sudden change of attitude towards him. He had expected the Italian to start putting on the pressure in Milan and this was why he had concentrated so hard upon retaining his usual composure against the odds. But the nervous tension of the flight had weakened his spirit and he felt too drained to keep up the pretence any longer.

'We didn't come all the way here to compare cars and their performance,' he rasped. 'Just use this one to get us where we're supposed to go.'

**See: The Revenger – Funeral Rites (Sphere Books)*

'Okay, Ralph,' Primo said, still grinning, as he fired the engine. 'There's no panic, though. We've got plenty of time.'

The Italian had a volatile temper and it would have been easy to give it free rein – to throw back, with interest, all the insults and innuendoes which Hooker had cast about him in the past. But Primo resisted the temptation. Hooker was having a bad time quelling his jangling nerves: offering him the opportunity to explode into anger might act as a release valve.

So, as Primo paid the parking fee and drove the sleek saloon away from the airport complex, he allowed his passenger to suffer in silence. There was sure to come a time, he thought, when the opportunity to repay old debts directly would present itself. He had waited so long to get his own back on the smug British bastard that he was prepared to delay his reprisal a little more – especially since he was able to kill the time in watching Hooker suffer as a result of a third party's actions.

As the Audi swung out of the airport precincts on to the road towards Antibes, a white Renault R8 with an Avis sticker on the rear window nosed forward from a parking space and juggled through the traffic to take up a position three vehicles behind the bronze-coloured car.

At the wheel was a tall, slimly-built man in his mid-twenties dressed in a conservatively casual garb of black trousers flared at the ankles, white shirt with rolled up sleeves and no tie. His face was long and lean, with deep-set, clear blue eyes, slightly concave cheeks and a gentle mouth line given character by an almost fully developed bandito moustache and strength by a resolute jaw structure. He had jet black hair just beginning to recover from a drastic cropping.

As one of the cars separating the Audi and the Renault veered away into a right turn, the driver of the R8 reached into the top pocket of the check-patterned sports coat on the passenger seat and drew out a pair of wrap-round Polaroid sunglasses. He settled them on the bridge of his nose and then dropped his hand back on to the coat. His exploring fingers probed for a side pocket and his thin lips cracked into a mirthless smile as he touched the reassuring smoothness of metal.

There was a fully-loaded Smith and Wesson 9mm. Automatic in the pocket. Every one of the bullets in the magazine had Ralph Hooker's name on it. For the driver of the Renault was Stark.

CHAPTER TWO

The road to Antibes had really started for Stark when he agreed to take part in the company-planned robbery of the Danton Electronics payroll. But a great deal had happened since then. Arrest, prison, break-out and bloody revenge against those responsible for the death of the only girl he had ever loved. And, at some point in the midst of all that, his decision – or realisation – that the trail of vengeance he had set out upon had no end – short of his own death. For the company could not allow a renegade like Stark to kill its employees and cripple its undercover operations without fighting back. So the word had been spread – get Stark and earn a twenty thousand pound bonus as well as the undying gratitude of the company.

As a marked man, he therefore had no alternative but to get the company before the company took him out. Once he had accepted this premise, his course of action was easy to plot, but less so to follow. For apart from the countless company men eager to earn the big bonus, he was also wanted by the police. And the official search for him was being led by Superintendent Evan Evans, who had a good and painful reason to hold a grudge against Stark. In addition, there could be few people in the United Kingdom who had not seen his photograph in newspapers and on television and were therefore aware of the thousand pounds reward offered by Danton Electronics.

But as Stark drove the hired Viva across the Thames on Putney Bridge he did not allow his unenviable position as the most wanted man in the country to worry him. He was on his way back to London from a suburban cemetery where he had shot dead one of the two men who actually killed Carol and watched as the second murderer was arrested by the police.

If he felt anything at all, it was a faint glow of satisfaction with, behind this, a sense of invincibility. In under two days he had shaken the company to its evil foundations and left egg – sometimes blood – on the faces of numerous humiliated policemen. But beneath this near euphoria in his mind were the jagged edges of grief for Carol and his dead parents and he knew with certainty that these would always be there: throwing deep shadows from his sub-conscious and reminding him of his avowed intention to crush the company.

The afternoon was drifting into evening and losing some of its warmth and spring brightness. The outward-bound rush hour had begun and he made good time against the flow of traffic. It was not until he was stopped by a red light in the Kings Road that he realised he had no destination in view: no specific plan of how to continue his campaign against the company.

The traffic lights were on the pavement outside a male boutique. When they changed to green, he turned the corner into a side street with parking meters on one kerb and double yellow lines opposite. All the meters were in use. He angled into the gutter and parked on the yellow lines. He shrugged out of his raincoat before he left the Viva and when he did get out he ignored the keys in the ignition. He kept his pace nonchalant as he walked back towards Kings Road, allowing the coat to swing freely from his arm. It was heavy with the weight of the Snub Magnum revolver in the pocket.

The boutique was called Brute Force. Inside, the light level was low, the air over-heated and redolent with the fragrance of incense, vibrant with progressive pop music.

'Can I help, darling?'

The voice was loud and high-pitched to reach through the sound barrier. It could have been male or female. When Stark looked at the figure approaching him, he was still not sure about the sex. Long hair, false eyelashes, high necked sweater stretched tight over a flat chest, and Oxford Bags too loose to offer any clue.

'Yourself to my money when I find what I want,' Stark answered, swinging towards a rack of trousers.

The assistant gave a shrug and a pout and retreated to the depths of the shop. Stark made his selections quickly, finding a pair of dark blue trousers, a pink shirt with matching tie, a slipover with a quiet pattern and a leather jacket with a minimum of trim. There was a curtained alcove to serve as a changing room and he used this to get out of his old clothes – which were featured in the official description of him – and into the new. The trousers had two side and two hip pockets and there were four pockets in the jacket. This had been a prime consideration in making his choice and he was able to stow away the revolver, passport in the name of Michael Hodder and over nine thousand pounds in assorted currencies without showing too many bulges.

He collected together the price tags he had taken from the clothes and totalled them up. Then he counted out enough money in British bank notes to cover the cost, gathered up his old clothes and stepped back through the curtain.

The assistant moved forward, face decorated by an admiring smile. 'Beautiful, darling.'

'I won prizes in baby shows,' Stark answered wryly, shoving the labels and money towards the assistant. 'At these prices you can afford to give me a bag for my old stuff?'

'Pleasure, darling.'

First, the money was counted and checked against the tags. Then a plastic bag was produced. As the assistant bent forward to help in packing the old clothes, Stark saw the bald patch on top of his head. He also noted the short stubble of a day's growth sprouting through the pancake on the jaw.

'I'll do it, sweetheart,' he said sarcastically, snatching the bag away. 'You look like you've had a hard time today. Why don't you relax with a fag.'

'Up yours!' the queer hissed malevolently as Stark pushed the clothes into the bag and headed for the door.

'You should be so lucky,' Stark shot back as he stepped out on to the pavement.

Sloane Square, with its Underground station, was a splash of green trees and lawn at the end of the grey street. He turned into two more shops before he reached the station – a pharmacy to buy a pair of wrap-round Polaroid sunglasses and a radio and TV store for a cheap transistor. Nobody except the assistants behind the counters paid any attention to him and their casual interest was merely professional.

The embryo moustache which was as yet only a black shadow over his top lip helped to alter his appearance a little. The dark-lensed glasses were a bigger contribution and the change of clothes made him feel better. But, as he rode on a westbound Circle Line train, he could see his reflection in the dark mirror of the window across the aisle and there was something about his image that struck a wrong note. He did not pin it down until the train rattled into Paddington station and screeched to a halt – the prison crop was in violent contrast to everything else about him.

When he reached street level it was after five-thirty and most of the shops were closed. But the owner of a sporting goods store was just finishing the chore of sweeping the entrance prior to putting up the shutters. The day had been a good one for business – the first warm one in a cold and damp spring. It had brought in customers clamouring for tennis racquets, golf clubs, cricket bats and a variety of other accoutrements for summer sports. The owner was unwilling to tempt providence by refusing a further sale so stayed open the minute longer it took Stark to find a cream golfing cap which fitted him.

The back streets of Paddington close to the main line station were well-served by guest houses and hotels ranging from close to star rating to the unashamedly seedy. Stark selected the Opal Hotel, which aimed at the lower end of the market. A sour-faced man, with a wheezing voice and skin that seemed to have been clinging to his frail body for more than a hundred years, did not even look up at Stark's face as he pushed forward the register and demanded two pounds fifty payment in advance.

Then he gave him a room key, told him to read the rules of the hotel which were pasted to the back of the door, and returned to his dull-eyed viewing of a children's quiz game on the portable TV perched at one end of the desk.

The hall and stairway to the first floor smelled of damp and diesel fumes. A door opened on a landing and a guilty-looking middle-aged man with a neatly folded raincoat and rolled umbrella emerged. He stopped short as he saw Stark, then gulped and rushed headlong down the stairs. In the room, a woman of thirty with unkempt hair and smudged make-up reached into the neckline of a torn nightdress and scratched her armpit.

'Either shut the door or come in, son,' she said as she sensed Stark watching her and looked up.

'I'm glad I have a choice,' Stark told her, pulling the door closed from outside.

She hissed something at him but he didn't catch it as he

moved down the landing and fitted the key into the lock of the door next to the prostitute's room. Inside, there was a token strip of carpet beside the single bed. The rest of the floor was covered by oilcloth, worn through to the boards in several places. The once pink wallpaper was stained to a light brown by cigarette smoke and time. The bed mattress was hard and the sheets had a grey tinge. The mirror on the dressing table was cracked in several directions and two dead flies were trapped by a spider's web in the built-in wardrobe. There was a venetian blind, heavily coated with dust, hung at the small window which overlooked a dustbin-crowded area to the blank wall of a printing works beyond. Flatbed letterpress machines thudded rhythmically.

Stark stripped the filthy quilt from the bed and stretched out on the slightly cleaner blanket beneath, using the boutique bag stuffed with his old clothes as a pillow. He switched on the transistor and held it on his chest as he listened to the six o'clock news headlines. The main item reported on the shoot-out between police and company men at the Surbiton cemetery. An outside broadcast unit had been sent to the scene of the shootings, where three men and a woman had been killed and a police detective slightly injured.

'. . . the police say,' the news reporter continued excitedly. 'One of the most puzzling aspects of this bizarre, Wild West type shoot-out, is concerned with the death of Frank Adams. He was out of both sight and range of police marksmen when he was killed – apparently trying to escape from the cemetery. And initial investigations suggest the bullet which entered his body was not fired from a gun normally issued to police officers.

'So we can assume – as one of the arrested men's lawyer's maintains – that the escaped convict John Stark took part in the Surbiton shootings and murdered Adams in cold blood. Police are not at this stage able to deny or confirm this. They are not even stating categorically that Stark tipped them off to the presence of gunmen at Surbiton.

'But what is certain is that Stark seems set upon destroying, single-handed, the highly sophisticated criminal organisation known to the police and underworld as "the company". For everything points to the fact that he has been responsible for the deaths of four men – not counting Adams – who had links with the company. And earlier today, speaking from a hospital bed, Superintendent Evan Evans, who is in charge of the hunt for Stark, revealed that the wanted man had tipped off police to the location of a company-owned laboratory used for processing raw opium into heroin.

'As reported in an earlier bulletin, the superintendent was admitted to hospital suffering from a broken arm, concussion and facial injuries sustained in an attempt to apprehend Stark this morning.

'The superintendent is quoted as saying that despite the fact that the wanted man is waging a war of revenge against the criminal organisation known as the company, he cannot be allowed to usurp the authority of duly constituted law and order, and every avenue is being explored with the aim of recapturing John Stark. The description of the wanted man issued by the police is as . . .'

Stark pressed the switch to turn off the radio and then lay still for several minutes, staring up at the grimy ceiling. He had learned nothing new from the newscast, except that Evans' injuries were not as serious as they might have been. He was glad of that, but unable to project what his reaction would have been had the detective been permanently maimed, or even killed. Stark had no real quarrel with Evans. The man had a job to do and was doing it as best he could. But then so did Stark, and if he had any chance at all of completing it, he had to be prepared to smack down every form of opposition, no matter from which quarter it came.

He spent six days at the Opal Hotel, paying the shrivelled, grasping man on the desk each evening for the night and day ahead. Most of the time he spent sleeping or listening to the radio. He never ate breakfast and bought his lunches and dinners from nearby fish and chip bars and take-away Chinese counters, smuggling the food up to his room. He ate double portions at every meal – treble when he could force it down. His stomach showed signs of fattening first, but then his cheeks began to swell and his jawline thickened. His moustache developed well and he trained it into a droop at each corner of his mouth. His black hair lengthened, but not as quickly as he would have liked. So he bought a bottle of grey tint from the barber who sold him the razor and lather, and added streaks of colour to the black.

The only new development in the search for him hinged on the discovery of the hired Viva off the Kings Road. It was traced to Sheri McShane, the girl killed by police in the Surbiton cemetery, and investigations were continuing.

It was a bright Sunday morning, almost eleven o'clock, when Stark went out of his dingy room, leaving behind only the dust and dirt which he had found there. He carried his old clothes and whatever remained of his local purchases in the plastic bag from the boutique. He paid the man on the desk for three more nights, knowing that nobody would be sent in to clean the room until the time bought by the money had expired – guests at the Opal Hotel were expected to look after themselves.

'Launderette,' he said as the old man looked inquiringly at the overstuffed bag.

'My old woman'll wash 'em for you cheaper,' the man behind the desk offered with an avaricious gleam in his watery eyes.

Stark shook his head. 'Thanks, but I have this thing about seeing the women put their bras and pants in the machines, dad,' he said.

The old man smacked his lips in distaste. 'Rose upstairs has told me about you kinky types,' he wheezed.

'But I'm quiet with it,' Stark answered as he moved out of the musty-smelling hallway into the tepid brightness of the morning.

He went down to Paddington Underground and took a Circle Line train to Baker Street, then changed to a southbound Bakerloo train and left it at Piccadilly Circus. The section of the carriage where he sat was empty except for a sleeping parson and he let the boutique bag stay where it was on the floor. When the bag was found its contents were certain to be traced to him but the police would have no means of knowing where he had got on or off the train.

Piccadilly Circus was crowded with early season tourists testing the legend that if you stood in the shadow of Eros for long enough, everybody you had ever known would pass by. Those who had grown bored with waiting took photographs of the God of Love, the never-ending circle of traffic and the drop-outs who either played guitars or tried to put the touch on the rich peasants.

Stark counted six uniformed constables either in the Circus or the streets spoking away from it. He did not push his luck by looking at any of them directly, but neither did he panic into ducking from sight. He simply waited patiently at a Green Line bus stop and pretended a passing interest in any halfway attractive woman who walked by.

The bus was a single-decker pay-as-you-enter, three-quarters full with more tourists. But these were entirely of the homegrown variety – mostly family groups heading for an afternoon in the country.

Stark paid his fare to Weybridge and found a vacant seat close to the rear of the bus. A fat woman with a vacuum flask and foil-wrapped packet of sandwiches on her lap stared hard at Stark as he sat down. But there was no sign of recognition or suspicion in her irate gaze. She merely resented having to share the seat.

It was almost two when he got off the bus. He stood at the stop and watched the bus start off down the road, then glanced around with distaste. He was city born and bred and could accept the country in small doses. But he detested the suburbs and everything about them. And he knew why. A suburb and the people who lived there were neither one thing nor the other. They were one big compromise and Stark considered compromise of any kind unworthy of respect.

He asked a man pushing a pram how he could get to St. George's Hill and was directed along St. George's Avenue and into the right fork of Egerton Road. As he followed the pram-pusher's instructions, Stark breathed in air heavy with a mixture of scents – Sunday roasts, car wax, fresh mown grass, spring flowers and money. This last became stronger the nearer he got to his destination. But it wasn't a smell, of course. He picked it up with his eyes as he saw the houses get larger and draw farther back into more expansive gardens surrounded by higher hedges.

He passed a sign proclaiming: PRIVATE ROAD – 25 MPH. He walked casually, strolling in the afternoon sun – a loaded revolver in his pocket. In his mind was a name and an address, blurted out by a girl to keep him from beating to death a queer. The queer had died anyway.

A white minivan with the name of a security company painted on the side crawled towards him, the sound of its engine in low gear silencing the birds in the conifers and birch trees flanking the road. Stark waved it down and a pair of stone-hard eyes surveyed him from under a cap vizor.

'I'm trying to find a house called Cottonwood,' Stark asked.

The eyes took in his youthful good looks and trendy clothes. They passed inspection. The days were long gone when the exclusiveness of St. George's Hill was exclusive only to pin-striped stockbrokers and company directors of middle and old age. The security man tried to guess whether Stark was a member of a pop group or a boy genius property developer. But he could just as well be an unwelcome sightseer.

'Who lives there?' the guard demanded.

'Ralph Hooker,' Stark answered easily.

CHAPTER THREE

Stark found the house within ten minutes by following the security man's directions. It was new, but built to look old in the manner of a Georgian country house. It stood, gleaming white in the sunlight, at the centre of a two acre plot of lawns and flowerbeds, the whole surrounded by an eight-feet high red brick wall. The only way in – unless anybody wanted to risk injury from the broken glass and barbed wire running along the top of the wall – was through a pair of wrought-iron gates at the start of a gravel driveway. Both gates were folded back along curves of well-oiled track which suggested they were powered by an electric motor.

The house, standing behind a turning circle of recently weeded gravel at the end of the driveway, looked deserted. All the windows were tightly shut and several were blinded by drape curtains. But the whine of a busy, low-power engine sounded from behind the house.

Stark moved along the driveway, his shoes crunching on the gravel, sounding as if he was walking on a crisp carpet of frozen snow. He worked at keeping his gait casual, but one of his hands, loosely resting in the pocket of his jacket, was curled around the butt of the short-barrelled ·357 Snub Magnum confiscated from a dead company man. And the easy movements of his head, swinging to left and right, were deceptive. For his narrowed eyes were alert for the first sign of a threat from the house or any section of the grounds.

He reached the pillared porchway without attracting any overt attention. The whine of the motor was louder now and he realised what it was as he picked up a strong smell of fresh-cut grass – an electric rotary lawnmower. He caught his breath, tightened his grip on the revolver and rang the door bell. It sounded far off, like a distant warning. But he ignored it, not needing to be reminded – in actuality or by his imagination – that he was taking a high risk.

But it was a calculated one. He was safe from the police here. In a time of serious trouble Leo Ryan had come running to Hooker for help. And since Ryan was a director of the company, that meant Hooker was a big fish which in turn meant he was clean as far as the police were concerned. For the continued operation of the company depended upon its highest echelon maintaining an unblemished front. He also guessed – and it could be no more than a guess – that Hooker would not feel the need to surround himself with company muscle and gunmen. For he doubted if Sheri McShane would have blown the whistle on herself by admitting to anybody that she pointed the finger at Hooker.

So Stark listened to the silence which answered the ring of the door bell and did not even consider the possibility that it was inviting him into a trap. He moved across the bay windowed front of the house and halted at the corner to peer along the side. There was a four-car garage with one of the up-and-over doors open to show a lot of empty space and an oil slick in the centre of the concrete floor.

A trellis archway entwined with bloomless rambling-rose plants linked the house with the end of the garage. Stark moved up close to this and looked through. The gardens at the rear were as well-tended, and more elaborate than those at the front, with stepping stone pathways connecting rose beds and arbors; a grass tennis court, a heart-shaped fish pond and a large greenhouse bursting with the colours of tropical flowers.

The man pushing the mower was a red-headed giant, several inches taller than six feet, with a thick torso and bulging legs and arms. He was dressed in a dark blue denim shirt and brown corduroy trousers. He protected his hairless head from the weak sun with a flat cap. He was cutting an area of lawn on the other side of the fishpond. Stark waited for him to reach the edge of a rose bed and turn around to go back the other way. Then he stepped through the trellis archway and made good time across the already close-cut lawn. He was level with the gardener and no more than thirty feet away from him when the giant swung around to start a new swathe. He concentrated upon keeping the trailing cable away from the blade and did not look up and see Stark until he had closed the gap by two feet.

'Here, what you think you're doing?' he demanded, his tone broad Cockney. He was about forty, with the ruddy complexion of an outdoor worker. He had a sullen mouth and dull eyes.

Stark thought he was as stupid as he looked and sounded. But he took no chance with the man's possible compensation of animal cunning: there was no doubting his brute strength. 'Pointing a gun at you – for now,' Stark replied as the gardener released the trigger on the electric mower and the whine ceased.

The man's dull eyes surveyed Stark's casual stance contemptuously. He looked ready – and entirely capable – of lifting the lawnmower and hurling it at Stark. 'You ain't funny, so piss off, mate!' he snarled.

Stark made a tutting noise with his tongue. 'You're a blot on this neighbourhood,' he accused. 'I think the people around here might take up a collection for me if I kill you.'

He withdrew his right hand from his pocket and pointed the Magnum at the gardener. The man gasped and took a startled step backwards. Stark took two paces forward. It was only just over a week ago that he had first handled a gun. In that time he had shot four men to death and wounded another. But he could still not bring himself to trust his aim over anything but the shortest range.

'You're bloody mad, mate!' the gardener accused.

'That's good,' Stark said evenly, cracking his thin lips into a smile, which did not reach his eyes concealed behind the dark glasses. 'You're willing to talk to me. Let's go over there and find something more interesting to discuss.'

He used his free hand to point to a cedarwood shed at one end of the greenhouse. The door was open and it was from here that the electric cable snaked to power the mower.

'Who the hell do you think . . .?' The gardener's expression suffered an abrupt switch from incomprehension to harsh surprise. 'Here, you're that geezer what . . . who's been doing all the . . . You're Stark!'

'That's good, Hulk,' Stark complimented with heavy sarcasm, then changed his tone to mimic the gardener's thick accent. 'The geezer what took out a lot of other geezers.' Now his tone changed again, this time to heavy menace and he backed it up with the hard line of his mouth and a probing motion with the gun. 'Seeing as how you're such a bright spark, Hulk, I'm anxious to talk to you. But I can probably find another genius with an even higher I.Q. than you. So before I put a hole in your head and dent that brilliant brain of yours, pick up the mower and get over there.'

The gardener hesitated for several stretched seconds while his mind digested what Stark had said and set it alongside the visual image of the pointing gun. He was forced to concede that Stark was not bluffing. He hoisted the mower with one hand and coiled the slack cable with the other as he moved woodenly towards the shed. He was within three yards of the open doorway when he whirled, swinging the mower in a far-reaching arc.

But he had made a wrong guess about Stark and when he saw his mistake, his ruddy face paled. Stark had seen the gardener's back and arm muscles grow tense as the shed came closer and predicted the attack. So he halted, widening the gap and waiting for the move. As the gardener whirled, Stark was standing like a statue, at least two feet out of range of the swinging mower, the gun tucked in close to his hip.

Once the attack was launched, it gathered too much momentum to halt. And, swinging free with every ounce of strength the gardener could muster, it unbalanced the big man. As he pivoted almost full circle and then staggered to the side, bending from the waist to steady himself, Stark shot him. He aimed low, for the legs. But the gun jolted and the gardener squealed and fell headlong as the bullet thudded into his meaty buttock.

'You bleeding bastard!' he rasped, letting go of the mower and reaching down at his wound with both hands.

'You're the one that's bleeding,' Stark pointed out lightly, stooping to set the mower upright and gripping the handle loosely in his free hand. 'But you're all right to talk still. We've already established you don't carry your brains in your arsehole. Get in the shed, Hulk.'

The gardener tried to rise, but it was a painful process and he was reduced to crawling over the threshhold into the shed. Stark followed him inside, carrying the mower. As the gardener rested full-length on the floor, alternately massaging his injury and examining the streaky blood on his hands, Stark gathered in the slack power cable and then closed the door.

It was a large shed, with two windows looking across

the sunlit greenery of the garden towards the house. There was a bench along one side lined with boxes and pots of seedlings beginning to sprout. Bags of lawn food and artificial fertiliser were stacked in one corner and gardening tools hung from racks on the walls. The shed had recently been given a fresh coating of preservative and the warm air was heady with the smell.

Stark glanced out of one of the windows towards the rear of the house. It looked as impassive as the front – every window and door tightly closed. But if there had been anybody inside they would probably have heard the shot. He doubted if the sound had carried over the boundary wall as more than an inoffensive thud. He looked down at the pained face of the gardener, and pushed the flexible peak of the golfing cap up against the crown. He wiped a line of sweat beads from his forehead with the back of a hand.

'Question and answer time, Hulk,' he announced pleasantly. 'Time to put your brilliant mind to the test.'

'Piss off, Stark,' the fallen giant flung at his tormentor.

Stark stepped casually forward, then swung his foot in a vicious kick. The toe of his shoe landed hard in the area of the gardener's kidneys and the man grunted. His agony showed as sweat oozed from every pore of his face.

'Stupid!' Stark chided. 'Where's the boss, mate?'

'Get stuffed.'

'Do better,' Stark instructed.

The gardener rolled over on to his side, his back coming up against the legs of the bench. Hate-filled defiance shone through the glaze of pain in his dull eyes. 'Go screw your mother' he grated.

The gardener knew the violent manner in which Stark's mother had died. Everybody knew it. But Stark fought the heat of his anger: his actions were unhurried and his face a mask of impassiveness as he reached out and curled his free hand around the grip of the mower handle.

'Jesus!' the gardener screamed as the motor was triggered into whining life.

He tried frantically to scuttle away as the mower was tilted on to its back roller and he saw the whirling blade thrust towards his face. But the bench legs were an unyielding barrier to retreat. He brought up his hands and covered his face.

Stark jerked the mower forward and heard his victim's scream above the unchanging note of the electric motor. Blood sprayed up, like rusty water from a ruptured pipe. When he switched off the mower and withdrew it he stared grimly at the skeleton hands of the gardener, stripped of flesh and gleaming white against the pulpy scarlet ground of exposed tissue.

'You touched on a sore point, Hulk,' Stark said softly as the gardener dropped his useless hands to the bare boards of the floor and began to whimper. 'Just answer the questions without making me see red.'

'Away,' the gardener said hoarsely. Some of the blood had splashed on his face. He licked a drop from his top lip. 'Mr. Hooker's gone away. That's all I know, so help me God.'

'For how long?' Stark wanted to know. 'The afternoon, the day, a week, a month?'

The man on the floor began to tremble with delayed shock. His entire face seemed to twitch – with the exception of his mouth. His lips stayed clamped shut in a firm line. Stark merely touched the mower trigger for an instant, whining the electric motor into brief life.

'I don't know!' the gardener yelled. 'He don't tell me what he does or where he goes. Why the bleeding hell should he?'

Stark believed him. The gardener was a broken man, incapable of lying. 'The gates are open and a car's missing from the garage,' he said with easy insistence. 'Hooker?'

The gardener tried to shake his head, but his neck muscles refused to co-operate. 'No,' he answered. 'Mrs. Hooker. He went yesterday. With a suitcase – like he was going away.'

'How about her?'

'What?'

'She'll be back, will she?'

'Pretty soon. Taken the twins back to boarding school. Only a few miles away.'

'That's good, Hulk,' Stark congratulated. 'Now you're showing how bright you really are. You should have been friendly from the start, instead of getting cut up about my interest.'

The gardener stared up imploringly at Stark and his

whole body began to tremble, the movement stopping only at the wrists of his useless hands.

'Do you know what the company is, Hulk?'

The gardener gulped. 'Yeah,' he whispered.

Stark shook his head sadly. But behind the masking lenses of the dark glasses, his blue eyes were diamond hard. 'And you work for the company, Hulk? You take care of the garden, but that's not your real job?'

'No.' The monosyllable was just an exhalation of breath with a hint of a negative in it.

'Your main purpose is to keep people like me away from Hooker?'

'Yeah.'

'That's bad, Hulk,' Stark said in a hushed tone. 'If somebody like me had got to Hooker a long time ago, Carol would still be alive.'

'Look, mister, I . . .'

The gardener's voice had risen, panic injecting a hysterical strength into it. But it trailed away as Stark pushed up the Polaroids to rest on his forehead, showing the man his eyes with the killer gleam in them.

'I'm looking and I see a murderer, Hulk,' Stark said softly. 'I hope you had a hearty breakfast.'

He squeezed the trigger of the revolver. The bullet spiralled into the left side of the man's chest. His eyes stayed open and there was just a token splash of blood from the wound. Death was instantaneous as the twisting lead smashed through the heart valves. The nervous system received the message and acknowledged with a violent judder. The gardener lay still.

Stark opened the door of the shed and listened. Birds sang and a blow-fly zoomed in over his shoulder to feed on the gardener's quick-drying blood. But the rich and beautiful people of St. George's Hill didn't get the scent. The insulating effect of their wealth was too strong to allow such unpleasantness to penetrate their carefully erected privacy.

CHAPTER FOUR

The Côte d'Azur was living up to the claims of the travel brochures. The season was not yet under way but already the beaches from Cap-Ferrat to Cap d'Antibes had taken on the colour of newly ripened wheat in the strong sunlight. To the south, the Mediterranean was an unending sheet of light and dark blue marred only by the white water of the wakes trailing the yachts heading for resort marinas and the tramp steamers churning towards Toulon and Marseilles. While to the north the Alpes Maritimes were gently on fire with the myriad colours and shades of sub-tropical blooms against the green and grey ground of the hill structure.

And it was towards the high ground rather than the shoreline that Enrico Primo headed the Audi when he turned off the A8 autoroute. The road ran straight for a mile or so up a gentle incline, flanked by shuttered villas at the edges of fields of lavender and rosemary, the verges lined by cypresses and olive trees. Then, as the foothills presented a more difficult barrier, the road began to snake in a series of sharp hairpin bends.

The Italian handled the car with casual abandon, enjoying the tight-lipped terror he saw on the face of Hooker as the nearside wheels of the Audi drifted towards the sheer drop at the start of many of the high bends.

'Pretty nice scenery, eh Ralph?' Primo shouted enthusiastically above the whine of the engine, taking a hand from the wheel and waving it expansively towards the broad valley.

'Put your hand back on the steering wheel, you idiot!' Hooker shouted in hoarse reply.

Primo laughed, eyes twinkling and teeth flashing against his tan at this discovery of yet another flaw in Hooker's shield of cool reserve. Primo had been born and raised in a mountain village of the Dolomites and towering heights held no dizzying terrors for him.

With Hooker's mind embroiled with a new cause for anxiety and the Italian enjoying his private joke, neither man had the time or inclination to check whether the

Audi had a tail. The last time Hooker had looked back over his shoulder had been on the autoroute where traffic had been too heavy to single out whether any particular car driver was showing interest in the Audi. Primo had watched the white Renault make the turn on to the side road but had seen nothing suspicious about this. It was a public highway that led to a great many places. And anyway, Primo was certain the Briton's fears were unfounded. Even if Stark was gunning for Hooker, he had no way of knowing about the Milan–Nice flight – and without company help, how could a man wanted so badly by the law get out of the United Kingdom?

No, Hooker's cool efficiency had been a sham. He was really nothing but an old woman – okay so long as operations ran smoothly, but a ratbag of nerves at the first sign of trouble.

At the wheel of the R8, Stark had no way of knowing the states of mind of Hooker and his companion. He could not even be sure that the chairman of the United Kingdom company was unaware his European itinerary had been revealed. So he took no chances. At the end of the straight stretch of road he slackened speed, allowing the leading car to widen the gap. Thus, for a great deal of the time, he lost sight of the Audi, catching only the occasional glimpse of it as the bronze bodywork and polished windows flashed sunlight at the apex of each hairpin.

But there was no risk of losing contact until the road crested the hill for there were no turn offs: just broad areas gouged out of the rock for tourists to park and drink in the spectacular mountain scenery. Hooker and the Italians were not tourists. But there were several sightseers using the parking areas and, as the Audi went from sight through the pass, a long coach and two Citroens pulled out on to the road ahead of Stark.

He gave a grunt of irritation and was forced to drop down to bottom gear as the coach struggled to haul its length around a bend. The Citroen drivers launched into a Continental duet of angry horn blowing and Stark made it a trio. The grinning coach driver ignored them as he spun his wheel, coming out of one bend and immediately angling across to the wrong side of the road to make the next turn easier. The Citroens, horns blaring on a single note and headlights blazing, raced by on the inside. As the coach driver and his passengers glared and hurled abuse, the cars went nose-down into the bend and side-slipped out.

Stark pushed the accelerator pedal to the floor and attempted to emulate the other drivers. But the eleven hundred engine of the Renault was only a little over half the size of the Citroen Super's power units and he had to stomp on the brake as the towering side of the coach swung across his path.

A *camion* and trailer rattled down in the opposite direction on the next straight section of road and he was unable to race ahead of the straining coach until the final hairpin before the pass. He crested the rise and raked his narrowed eyes over the new vista spread before him. The valley continued, curving around to the west and narrowing as the sides steepened. The road maintained a steady altitude with a sheer drop on one side, protected by a concrete wall, and conifers growing thickly on the slope of the rising ground towards the mountain ridge on the other. The sun was still high above the jagged line of the ridge so that only the very foot of the valley was in shadow. The road was bathed in brilliance, emphasising its emptiness.

Stark pushed the little car to its limit – then past it as the speedometer needle registered a hundred and thirty-five kph on a slight downward incline. The road had bends, but these were seldom fierce and Stark drifted the car around most of them with hardly a need to stroke the brake pedal – driving at speed was one of the few things at which he considered himself an expert.

Ten minutes passed before he saw a flash of sunlight on glass far ahead. The trees on his right whipped by as a blur of subdued colour as he kept the Renault travelling at its limit, closing the gap. The road ahead swung to the left, skirting a thrusting cliff of white rock and he recognised the shapes of the two Citroens silhouetted darkly against the lighter ground of the cliff face. Their brake lights splashed timidly in the brightness of the sun as they slowed for the bend around the outcrop. Then both cars went from sight.

Stark kept his foot hard down around the outswinging bend, then hit the brakes and wrenched on the wheel as the concrete barrier loomed in his path. The body shell canted sharply and the inside rear wheel lifted. Coolly, handling the controls with gentle precision, Stark eased up on the brake pedal and adjusted his steering line a fraction. Then the wheel was inched over again and the car responded, tyres screeching and engine roaring.

The end of the rear bumper carved a shallow rut along the concrete barrier then hooked around the exposed loop of a metal reinforcement bar. It was torn free of its mountings and clanged into the road as the car raced out of the bend. A van coming in the opposite direction flashed its headlights, but Stark ignored it, his eyes focussed along the snaking black road which dropped in a series of gentle bends towards the small village at the head of the valley. There were perhaps four or five miles of roadway clearly visible and Stark could pick out a score of vehicles crawling up or edging down the hillside.

He pulled over to the side of the road and stopped, sliding out to stand on the parapet and survey the vista without the need to divide his concentration. There was no sign of the bronze car in which Hooker rode as a passenger. He checked a second time, after pushing the sunglasses up on to his forehead. Then he examined those sections of road partly obscured by stands of trees and the occasional house, making sure the Audi did not suddenly drive into view.

It was as he was making this third check that a flash of sunlight on a bright object showed on the periphery of his vision. He tried to pin-point it but could get no closer than a lush green area of pine trees. Then he spotted some wisps of grey wood smoke against the tree tops and wondered if it was one of these fire traces he had seen. His blue eyes, showing a hint of irritation, changed their focus and he looked at a pink-walled building at the edge of the road halfway along the tree line of the pine wood. A cluster of gaily coloured umbrellas at the side of the building suggested it was a bar or café.

Stark nodded suddenly, reaching a decision. He returned quickly to the Renault and shot it forward, heading down the side of the valley. As he neared the building with the pink-washed walls he saw that it was indeed a café – *La Vallée Vue*. There was a small parking space at one side but none of the cars on it was an Audi. Just the two black Citroens, an Innocenti Mini with Italian number plates and a German registered Skoda. On the other side of the split-level building was a small garden with metal tables and chairs set out beneath the sun umbrellas.

As Stark slowed the Renault he noted that one of the outside tables was being used by two men. A slim girl with jet black hair was serving them coffee. On the other side of the plate glass window offering a spectacular view along the length of the valley towards a patch of blue sea at the far end, the interior of the café was empty. Stark spun the wheel suddenly and turned on to the parking area. As he switched off the engine and lifted his coat from the seat, taking care the gun did not slip from the pocket, he glanced with guarded interest towards a rutted track that led away from the rear of the parking space and plunged into the pine wood. The ground was baked hard and there was no way to tell whether a car had recently added its weight to the old ruts sunk into the bare earth across the grass.

But Stark was not relying simply on a hunch that the Audi had turned off the road at this point. Logically, bearing in mind the time and distance picked up by the bronze coloured car near the head of the pass, this would have been the point it had reached shortly before Stark skidded around the final sharp bend and got a virtually unobscured view of the road down to the village. Add to that the four cars – excluding the Renault – parked beside a café which had only two customers and the result came up as a smell of excitement under Stark's nose.

He got out of the car, raking his gaze across the thickly growing trees on each side of the track. But there was nothing to see except dark trunks thrusting upwards from dense undergrowth. A flight of concrete steps rose up from the parking area to a narrow balcony along the front of the café. There was an open doorway at the side of the expanse of plate glass and he went through this, into a cool half-light reeking of strong French tobacco, Cognac and disinfectant. Then, as he sat down at a corner table from which he could look out on to the garden, he realised it wasn't disinfectant at all – just the natural perfume of growing pine trees drifting into the café from an open window at the rear of the building.

The waitress approached the table with dragging feet and a bored expression on her pretty face. But as he turned towards her and she saw his cool good looks, she brightened.

'Monsieur?'

Stark eyed her from head to foot from behind the shields of the dark glasses. She was near the end of her teens, perhaps had gone over the top into her twenties. Her slimness was deceptive, for close up she had interestingly thrusting breasts and generously curved hips. Perhaps she knew this and was proud of it, or perhaps she could not afford to buy a new black uniform sweater and skirt to give her developing figure room to fill out. When Stark's masked eyes settled upon the pouting prettiness of her face, he decided she wore the tight-fitting outfit for the effect it produced. For her dark eyes and moist lips suggested that she was available to serve more than drinks and food.

'Café, s'il vous plaît,' he said in heavily accented English grammar school French.

'Blanc?' Her eyes said a great deal more.

Stark shook his head. *'Noir.'*

'You are English, *monsieur*?' Her English was far better than his French.

'It shows, does it, darling?' he asked, cracking his lips in a grin.

She laughed. 'Sounds – in the fractured French.'

She whirled around and moved behind the espresso machine, accentuating the sway of her hips as she walked between the tables. Stark looked out of the window at the two men seated at the table beneath the shade of the umbrella. They were both in their mid-twenties, slimly built and over six feet tall. They had a kind of mid-thirties good looks – clear-eyed, soft-mouthed and slick-down-hair like the good guys in old style black-and-white gangster films. But a tell-tale bulge just below the shoulder at the front of each of their well-cut light blue suit jackets suggested to Stark that they were not the good guys at all.

The waitress returned with his coffee and leaned forward with an exaggerated bow to set the cup and saucer in front of him. One of her breasts nudged his upper arm. It felt firm and highly charged.

'Will that be all, *monsieur*?'

He smiled at her, responding to the not so veiled offer. 'Can you pack me up a couple of sandwiches and take the cork out of a bottle of wine?'

'Monsieur?'

'The smell of pine is good for my sinuses,' he explained. 'It's a nice day. A picnic in the woods behind the café seems like a great idea.' He brightened his smile. 'Make enough for two if you can get time off.'

Her face clouded and she shook her head emphatically, dismissing the entire plan. *'C'est pas possible, monsieur!'*

'Pourquoi pas?' Stark wanted to know.

'It is – how you say – private property.'

Stark thought it might be. 'There are no signs.'

She nodded in agreement. *'Oui, monsieur.* The former owner, he did not mind. There is only an ancient farmhouse on the property. Empty for many years. But the estate has been purchased. Nobody is allowed into the pine woods now.'

'That's a shame,' Stark muttered, and something in his tone aroused a new kind of interest in the girl – of a sort that had nothing to do with his sexual attractiveness.

She dragged her feet as she moved away, going back behind the counter. Her attempt to appear bored was too pointed as she ran a damp cloth along sparkingly clean shelves. She cast several surreptitious glances through the side window on to the garden. The men with guns in shoulder holsters continued their surveillance of the road. Their coffee cups were empty but they showed no inclination to order more. Eventually, the waitress reached a decision.

She was halfway to the door, still holding the cloth, when she sensed Stark watching her. She felt it necessary to explain. 'It is nicer out in the sunlight, *monsieur.*'

Stark grinned. 'I wouldn't know,' he said easily. 'I've never had it that way.'

The obscure English joke confused her. She shrugged, smiled wanly and drifted out of the café. Stark watched her without seeming to, as she moved from one table to another, running the cloth over them. It took her less than a minute to reach the table where the two gunmen sat. Her lips hardly moved as she spoke to them. The men glanced guardedly up at the side window and were in time to see Stark finish his coffee and rise.

Stark smiled out into the garden, raised a hand in farewell and rattled some coins in the saucer. Then he went through the doorway and down the steps into the parking area.

A Toyota Corona with Spanish number plates swept in off the road and dropped down into low gear as it bounced along the track between the trees. The fat man at the wheel wore a worried frown. Stark guessed he was late for an appointment.

He got into the overheated interior of the Renault and made a careful three-point turn. Out on the road, he headed down towards the village. One of the Citroens showed in his rearview mirror and hung there like an annoying spider on the back window. Stark's lips curled to show his teeth in a tight smile.

CHAPTER FIVE

Stark guessed that Cottonwood would be protected by a burglar alarm. And he knew Hooker could afford to have the best of everything. He wasn't about to start tampering with the possibly highly sophisticated beam, pressure and wire devices with which the house was likely to be fitted.

So when he left the shed with its grisly contents, he crossed to the garage block rather than the house. He stayed at the back, squatting down in the shadow of the wall, the gun held loosely in both hands, swinging to and fro between his knees. If he peered with great concentration across the partially cut lawns he could make out the shape of the gardener's legs and feet in the gloomy interior of the shed. But he didn't spend much time doing this. That particular man's contribution to the company had been brought to an abrupt halt. It was now time to consider his next, much bigger target.

He did not have to wait very long – less than half-an-hour before the quiet grounds of Cottonwood were invaded by the whisper of a powerful engine, giving only a fraction of its potential, and the crunch of gravel beneath slow-turning tyres. Stark stood up and inched along the wall. As he put an eye to the trellis with its covering of thick-growing foliage he was in time to see a brand new MGB swing off the driveway and angle towards the open garage. He ducked back into solid cover and waited, listening.

The car's engine note changed as it resounded in the confined space of the garage: then it died with no run-on. A door opened and closed and high heels clicked on concrete. The up-and-over panel folded down on well-oiled tracks and then the high heels crunched gravel as Judith Hooker walked towards the front of the house. She hummed tunelessly.

Stark waited until he heard the slam of the front door, then moved away from his hiding place. He trod lightly on the gravel chippings, but could not avoid making some noise. As he stepped up on to the pillared porch, an electronic buzz and a low squeaking signalled the remote controlled closing of the gates. He pressed the mother-of-pearl button set into the doorframe.

Judith Hooker took only a moment to open the door. and then backed away in shock. Stark eyed her with cool detachment as he stepped across the threshold, holding the gun in a loose grip, pointing in her direction rather than at her. She was a tall, slim woman probably in her late thirties and well preserved. She didn't have much of a figure but there was a certain lithe sexuality in the way she held her body. Her legs were good. The bone structure of her face was finely sculptured, with a hint of the Oriental in her high cheekbones and well-rounded jaw. Her eyes were jade green, complemented by the expensive blonde of her shoulder-length hair. She wore a toning green one-piece dress, buttoned from high neckline to hem and buckled at the wrists. The fit was designed to hint at her shallow curves without emphasising their meagreness.

'Hello, beautiful,' Stark greeted easily, closing the door behind him. 'Just keep co-operating like this and life will be that much easier – death, too, maybe.'

The initial shock of seeing a gunman on her doorstep had worn off: the numbness gone. Terror aged Judith Hooker ten years and she staggered, coming up hard against the umbrella stand.

'What . . . ?' was all she managed to blurt out.

'The name's Stark. Your husband has probably mentioned me, Mrs. Hooker.' He waved the revolver negligently. 'This isn't a sample. I'm not the Fuller gun salesman.'

The woman's attitude surprised Stark, for her fear did not deepen at the mention of his name. Then he realised she had probably recognised him the moment she opened the door. She seemed to read his thoughts and hurriedly denied his inference.

'I don't know . . . My husband isn't here. What do you want?'

Her knuckles were white where her hand gripped the umbrella stand, taking most of her weight. An air-conditioning unit hummed softly. It was cool in the sumptuously decorated hallway. A line of perspiration showed along the woman's top lip. The revolver gave off a faint smell of burnt cordite.

'Information, Mrs. Hooker,' Stark replied softly. 'For

a start, I'd like to know when you expect to have Mr. Big back in your bed.'

She fought to bring herself under control. It was not easy. She was out of practice. After fifteen years of marriage to Ralph Hooker she had grown used to a life of composed contentment. For her husband placed her on a pedestal and did everything in his power to ensure that she would not be afflicted by the trials and tribulations which cast shadows across the lives of less fortunate mortals. And since Hooker wielded a considerable amount of power, few were the occasions when trouble intruded on to the unruffled calm of his wife's cloistered existence.

'Why do you want to know?' she demanded, finding the strength to stand erect without support and the spirit to put force behind the words. Both qualities were summoned from a long way out of the past – from the twenty-five years she had got by before Ralph Hooker married her and introduced her to the cottonwool-wrapped, Cellophane-packaged Shangri-La of his own creation.

'My business,' Stark replied.

She spun around suddenly and paced across the hallway, entering the spacious, sunlit living room. She walked directly to a small corner table supporting the telephone and scooped the receiver off the cradle.

'I'm going to call the police,' she announced resolutely, her finger very stiff as she prodded the dial. 'I don't believe that's a real gun.'

Stark moved across the room with an unhurried gait. Mrs. Hooker flattened herself against the wall, but continued to dial. Her finger began to tremble. Stark picked up the base of the telephone.

'Your gardener knows it is,' he said softly, then jerked his arm back.

The woman gasped. The connecting wire was torn free of the junction box and the receiver leapt from her hand. Stark pivoted, his eyes peering through the dark lenses of the sunglasses, seeking a target. He spotted one and hurled the telephone. Judith Hooker screamed. The base of the instrument crashed into an ornate mirror hung on the wall above the false fireplace. The receiver, trailing the wire, smashed against the face of a clock on the mantelshelf. Gleaming shards of glass showered across the York stone hearth. The clock and telephone plunged down on top, powdering some of the fragments.

'I used to be a nice quiet fellow, Mrs. Hooker,' Stark said evenly as the woman tried to penetrate the barrier of his dark glasses and see his eyes. 'But people change. Mostly they're changed by other people. Your husband changed me. Where is he and when will he be back?'

The strain was too great and the time lapse too long. She was here now, in the present, living a waking nightmare in her home which for so many years had been inviolate to evil from behind its rich walls. The room swayed before her eyes and she saw the familiar objects of her surroundings in a strange new light. Then, as her eyes rolled up and her lids drooped, she saw nothing. She felt no pain as her knees bent and she pitched to the thick pile carpet in a dead faint.

'Oh, Christ!' Stark rasped.

But he did not allow this unexpected turn of events to delay his intention for more than a few moments. He ripped the wire loose from the telephone base and quickly, efficiently, tied up the unconscious woman. She had collapsed in such a manner that he did not have to rearrange her posture. First he bound her ankles together, then used the same length of wire to tie her wrists behind her back, forcing her arms out straight and dragging her feet tight against her lean buttocks. She looked uncomfortable, but her breathing was normal and she was unaware of what had happened to her.

He moved quickly through the ground floor of the house, taking impassive note of the blatant signs of wealth allied to good taste which featured in every room. Upstairs it was the same. Throughout the whole place the comfort and luxury was neutral, offering no clue to where the money had come to afford it. There was only one locked door in the house, this leading off the hallway at the front. There was a bunch of keys hanging in the formica and stainless steel kitchen, but none fitted the locked door. He went out on to the porch and tried to look in through the Georgian window with its mixture of plain and bubbled glass. The drape curtains were drawn.

He checked the cylinder of the revolver, pushing it out of the frame. Five of the six bullets had been fired. He threw the empty cases on the gravel and went around to the rear of the house, not sure that a single bullet would smash the lock and unwilling to waste his last one. He smelled death while he was still several yards from the shed. Inside, it was stronger as the trapped heat worked speedily at the decomposition process. The single blowfly had been joined by a score more of its kind. They buzzed away in an angry flock as Stark crossed to the tool rack and lifted down a twenty-pound sledge hammer.

It seemed to have doubled its weight by the time he carried it back into the hallway. In the living room, Judith Hooker groaned. Stark lifted the hammer and swung it. It smashed heavily on to the door handle. The handle dropped to the carpet and rolled. The door was still firmly locked. He gritted his teeth and thudded the hammer home again, and again, and again. As the head struck for the sixth time, the door burst open.

'What's happening?' the woman called plaintively from the living room.

Stark crossed the hallway and framed himself in the doorway. The woman pressed her trussed body hard against the wall as she stared at him, terrified at the sight of the enormous hammer he hefted with both hands.

'You want to tell me what I want to know before I have to smash up the whole house looking for it?' he asked evenly.

'Please,' she begged. 'I can't. My husband keeps his business and private lives completely separate. He's gone away on business. He never tells me anything about that part of his life.'

'Dangerous way to run a marriage,' Stark said. 'Keep quiet or you're dead, lady.'

Judith Hooker squeezed her eyes tight and tried to imagine it was not happening to her. That was how she had been able to withstand the agony of the twins' birth – the only occasion in her married life when her husband had been unable to guard her against pain and unpleasantness.

Stark left her to it and carried the hammer into the study. He jerked the curtain pull and flooded the room with bright sunlight. The decor was deep brown and gilt-edged – very masculine. The desk was mahogany with three drawers on each side. Each had a lock on it, but Hooker obviously considered the barrier of the door sufficient to protect his privacy from a cowed wife and over-indulged children. That an uninvited guest should get this far was unthinkable.

The drawers held stationery and printed matter referring to Drake Enterprises Limited. Stark had heard about the company – in the same way he knew of ICI, Esso, Barclays Bank and Woolworth. It was something of a surprise to see that the stationery listed Ralph Hooker as Chairman of Drake Enterprises. But he didn't waste time considering the implications, short of realising the organisation had to be the front for the company's activities. Crime on the gigantic scale of the company could not exist without a carefully constructed cover operation to explain the wealth and success of those who profited by it.

Then, as he turned away from the desk, Stark saw Ralph Hooker for the first time – depicted in a full-length oil painting hanging on a strip of wall between two narrow bookcases. Up until this moment, the man had merely been a name – a string of letters, a cypher, an idea to hate and to want to kill. But now Stark stood in front of the painting and studied it, imprinting the image upon his mind's eye of a tall, slim man in a two hundred pound suit cut on conservative lines, smiling down on the room with an arrogant mouth line and eyes which were only pretending. The artist had seen something behind the false expression in those grey, pebble-like eyes but had been unable – or unwilling – to show what it was.

When he was certain he had a deep enough impression to be able to recognise Hooker the moment he saw him, Stark noticed that the picture frame was held flush against the wall. He discovered the reason – it was hinged at one side instead of being hung from a cord. Stark tugged at the frame and the whole picture folded back against the side of one of the bookcases. He cursed as he saw the rectangular door of the safe with a combination lock dial sunk in the centre. He didn't know the first thing about safe-cracking and guessed this one would need a top-class professional to get inside it.

But his irritation didn't last for long. For he realised that whatever the safe held, it was unlikely to contain the answers to the particular questions that were on his mind.

So he returned to the desk and found them there. Arrayed neatly on the desk top was a strip lamp, a telephone extension, a penset, blotter and diary. And there it all was, in a neat, almost copperplate script:

Saturday: Milan, check-in Heathrow, five-thirty.

Three blank sections, then:

Wednesday: with Primo to Nice. Conference at three.

Beneath this entry, Hooker had doodled a halfway good picture of an airliner and written *Ug, not again!*

In the next section:

Thursday: Home.

The entries were made in blue with a felt-tipped pen. When Stark ripped out pages there were no tell-tale impressions left in the diary. He pushed the pages into his pocket, lifted the hammer and carried it out of the study. He crossed the hallway with its low hum of the air conditioner and into the living room. Judith Hooker had not moved. And as she heard Stark's return all she did was pop open her eyes. It was enough to show her naked terror.

'I know where he's gone,' Stark said.

She swallowed hard. 'Where?'

'If he didn't want you to know, he had a reason.'

'What has he done to you?'

'Blighted my young life,' Stark replied, preoccupied as he glanced around the rich furnishings of the room. 'You really don't know his plans, do you?'

'I told you. Ralph doesn't bring his work home with him.'

'How do you know when he's due back?' Stark asked.

'He'll telephone me from the airport. Please, what are you going to do?' Her voice was pleading, her eyes imploring.

Stark failed utterly to react. He pointed to a baby grand piano which dominated one corner of the room. 'Who plays that?'

She looked where he was pointing. Helpless as she was, she was willing to attempt any ploy to placate Stark's ice-cold, undemonstrative anger. 'It's Ralph's,' she said, trying for an even tone and almost reaching it. 'It relaxes him to play. He's teaching the twins.'

Then she gasped, realising her mistake. Stark approached the highly-polished piano slowly, the hammer swinging easily from both hands. Then he lifted it high and crashed it down on the centre of the keyboard. The ivories splintered as the instrument emitted a discordant death rattle. Again and again the hammer rose and fell, each new cacophony of tortured strings causing a spasm to race through the woman's body. In between, she stared at Stark's expressionless face, seeing not a single trace of enjoyment. It was just wanton destruction. When the keyboard was a complete wreck, Stark thudded the hammer down on to the lid and released his grip on the handle. The wood dented but did not crack. He sucked in a great breath and turned towards the woman on the floor.

'Why?' she asked from out of her shock.

'Carol always wanted to be a concert pianist,' he said, not really talking to Judith Hooker as he spoke aloud his thoughts. 'She wasn't that good, but she deserved better than the second-hand upright she had.'

'Will doing what you just did help her to get something better?' Judith Hooker asked, her voice rising.

Stark jerked himself out of his morbid train of thoughts. 'Nothing can help the dead, lady,' he said coldly.

The woman looked at him through a long silence. 'Are you saying that somebody you loved is dead and you blame my husband for it?'

'Come Wednesday you'll know the feeling,' he told her as he crossed to the door. 'You won't look at all bad in black.'

'Come back, please!' she screamed at him as he went out into the hallway. 'Please come back. Perhaps I can help?'

She went on, her tone rising to a hysterical pitch so that what she was saying became incomprehensible. Stark was not listening, anyway. Across from the umbrella stand was a table with a mirror above it. A bunch of keys rested on the table top. Set into the wall near the mirror was a switch panel, each toggle clearly labelled. He flicked down the one marked GATE and, as he stepped out through the front door, tossing the keys up and down, the gates at the end of the driveway swung open.

He drove the MGB out of the garage, through the gateway and south from St. George's Hill, his appetite whetted by the senseless attack on the inanimate piano. But soon he blanked out what had already happened and blotted the anticipation of what was to come. He was at the wheel of a fast car again and he allowed the pure enjoyment of this condition to take command of him.

CHAPTER SIX

The Citroen dropped back and went from sight long before Stark drove the Renault into the village. The clock on the belfry of the tiny church in the square showed that the time was three minutes past three and he recalled the note in Hooker's desk diary. But he did not hurry, deciding that the chairman of the British company would not fly from London to Nice via Milan to attend a meeting that would end almost as soon as it began.

He drove slowly around the square, sounding the horn at the picture-taking tourists, then out on to the road which climbed up the valley side towards the café at the edge of the pine wood. But he did not make a complete return journey. The northern fringe of the trees was out of sight of the café, concealed by a bend in the road. There were yellow no-parking lines painted on the heat-sticky tarmac, but he ignored them as he stopped the Renault and climbed out.

The driver of a bus bound for Cannes shouted and shook an angry fist at Stark as he was forced to swing to the wrong side of the road at the sharpest section of the bend. Stark grinned cheerfully and waved in response. Then he raised the lid on the rear mounted engine, waited until the road was clear of traffic and moved into the cool shade of the pine trees.

There were no well-trodden pathways among the towering pines and the brush became thicker as he moved deeper into the wood. The advantage of shade was soon lost as the battle for a passage through the prickly undergrowth bathed his body in sweat.

Once he was out of sight and earshot of the road his progress was slowed even further. For he was aware of the risk of losing his way among the trees, every one of which looked identical to his metropolitan-trained eyes. So there could be no wavering to left or right around particularly dense growths of brush. His chosen course was a diagonal line which he judged would bring him out on the track at least five hundred metres up the hill behind the café.

Then, suddenly, he reached this initial objective. He

ducked under a thorny overhang, stepped over a twisted root and halted with a sharp intake of breath. He had taken off his sunglasses so that he could wipe sweat from his eyes and now he blinked against the stab of bright sunlight unfiltered by foliage. He was at the top of a grassy bank which fell away sharply for six feet to the edge of the track. He drew back, sinking into a crouch and fumbled the gun from his pocket with sweat-greased fingers.

But there was no shout and no shot. He had not realised the need for stealth so quickly and he stayed on his haunches for long moments, until his pulse rate slowed to normal and his breathing quietened. By that time he knew that if the meeting place was guarded by more than the two sentries stationed at the café, they were not in the immediate vicinity.

He put the glasses back on and peered through the overhang, raking his eyes first one way and then the other along the track. Nothing moved within the restricted range – blocked off in both directions by sharp bends. Unless he was prepared to make the effort, and the noise, of battling through more undergrowth he had to show himself on the track, for the brush was a dense barrier to the top of the bank on both sides.

Then he became aware of the smell of woodsmoke with an underlying aroma of fresh coffee permeating the strong pine scent from the trees. This sign of the proximity of his objective decided his course of action and he straightened up, stepped over the root and half ran, half staggered down the bank. He worked the mechanism of the automatic to pump a shell into the breech and started up the slope of the track, keeping to the inside curve of the bend.

It swung to the right and then, more sharply, to the left. He crossed over and slowed his stride as the aroma of percolating coffee became stronger. The bank got steeper, but lower, and after a few more paces he halted abruptly, flattening himself against the almost vertical side of the track and peering through brush and tree trunks towards the house which had come into view.

It was a two-storey timber structure with an exposed chimney climbing the wall at one end and it was from here that the wood smoke whisped into the sunlit air. The house stood in the centre of a clearing, mostly hard-packed earth with tufts of tough grass sprouting here and there. The Audi in which Hooker and the Italian had arrived, together with the Madrid registered Toyota and a Pontiac Parisienne with French plates, was parked in the clearing fronting the house.

The house itself had once been a part of a thriving citrus fruit farm, but time and neglect had taken their toll. The timbers were warped and rotting, there was not a single whole pane of glass in the windows and the front door had come off its hinges and rested against the railed steps leading up on to the veranda which ran along half the length of the frontage. Behind the house, spread across a wide plateau which was like a single enormous step on the side of the valley, were several orange and lemon groves planted with trees which had become stunted and diseased from lack of care: the grass between them high and entwined with weed.

Stark inched further along the track, until the bank was low enough to allow him to step up without effort. On one side of the clearing was a barn in a worse state of disrepair than the house and he moved cautiously towards this. There was just a layer of springy ferns among the trees here and he was able to stay out of sight of the house a great deal of the time, darting from trunk to trunk. Then the blanket cover of the long barn protected him and he was able to make fast progress to the far end.

He felt it reasonably safe to assume that the men inside the farmhouse were relying solely upon the gunmen down at the café to keep out intruders. Certainly there were no sentries posted in the clearing and as he moved along the fringe of the open space he kept careful watch on the unglazed windows. He saw movement in the shadowed interior of only one room – on the ground floor at the chimney end of the house, beyond the reach of the veranda. But the man he saw was in the depths of the room, too far back to maintain a surveillance over the clearing.

The barn ended six feet short of butting on to the corner of the house in a right angle. Stark inched forward, gun extended, ears straining to pick up the slightest sound from the glassless window of the occupied room. There was a low murmur of conversation, but the words were indistinct against the discordant chorus of chirping crickets and buzzing of other insects. He went up on to the balls of his feet and reached the corner of the house in two long strides. He flattened himself against the wall and snaked around the corner, halting short of the window frame.

The conversation was in English.

'. . . Mr. Hooker,' a man said as Stark was at last close enough to hear clearly. 'You have seen the merchandise. And you have my guarantee that the bulk cargo is up to the standard of the sample.'

Stark pushed a finger and thumb up under his glasses and rubbed the saltiness of sweat beads from the corners of his eyes. Then he made an impulsive decision, pushed the glasses up on to his forehead and swung around. He had the automatic ready, but it wasn't needed. He peered into the room for a split second and then pulled his head back, the fleeting impression fixed in his mind.

It was the kitchen of the house. On one side was an enormous, old-fashioned solid-fuel range in which logs burned, bubbling coffee in two pots standing on the hot plate. Cupboards and shelves took up all the space on the two other walls he had seen. In the centre of the room was a large, rectangular table of seasoned pine which had not been scrubbed in many years. Six men sat around this on tubular metal chairs of the type used in the café down on the edge of the road. The two positioned to have a view through the window were Hooker and the man Stark recognised as his travelling companion from Milan. But both were concentrating on what was being said by the driver of the Toyota who sat at the head of the table.

Unaware that a man who had sworn to kill him was in a perfect position to do so at the very next instant, Ralph Hooker sighed and ran a hooked finger around the inside of his stiff shirt collar. He was not happy with the arrangements for the meeting and reacted by being obstructive.

He felt, with justification, that he had achieved a certain position within the company: had reached a status when he should no longer be required to discuss business in such primitive surroundings as this. The entire south coast of France was, in his estimation, comprised of little else except top class hotels – any one of which could have been used for this meeting in perfect safety. But the arrangements had been made by Jean-Claude Marette, whose cautiousness was something of a joke among top executives of the company. So, Hooker was bound to admit to himself, he should have expected something like this.

But this knowledge did little to appease his chagrin as he smelt the coffee and did some wishful thinking about a long gin-sling served on a balcony cooled by a sea breeze. And his mood was unimproved by the fact that his presence here was not strictly necessary. It was the Italian arm of the company which was in the market to buy the shipment of Armalite rifles which had disappeared six months previously from a supply depot in South Vietnam – and which was now in the holds of a Barcelona-registered freighter ploughing through the Straits of Gibraltar.

Thus, the only participants directly involved in the negotiations were Enrico Primo and the man responsible for stealing the guns, Manuel Vega. But Vega had been preceded to the meeting place by a taciturn bodyguard and Marette – present as a representative of the company in whose territory the meeting was taking place – had brought a lieutenant with him. Hooker's role at the farm was merely that of an arbitrator in the event of a disagreement. For the price tag on the automatic rifles was somewhere between one-hundred-and-fifty and two hundred thousand dollars American. And with that kind of money involved, the company's international board wanted to ensure they got a cast-iron return for their investment.

Nobody in the fetid kitchen of the farmhouse suspected for a moment that there would be a double-cross – Hooker included. Vega – short, barrel-chested and blue-jawed – was not a company man. But he was big as an independent arms salesman, well aware of with whom he was dealing and knowing what would happen to him and his organisation if he did not deliver the goods as specified.

But since Hooker was present, and already extremely uncomfortable, he felt it essential to his ego to assert himself even though it entailed prolonging his own ordeal as well as that of the others.

'I doubt nothing about the quality of the shipment, *señor*,' Hooker said as Marette got wearily to his feet and moved to the range. 'But the price is high.'

Vega glanced at Primo, who shrugged and listened attentively to the sound of the Frenchman pouring coffee into six chipped mugs. The Spaniard turned his eyes to the smoke-blackened ceiling, struggling to keep his volatile temper under control. He didn't like the tall, gaunt-faced Englishman and was aware that the feeling was mutual. 'Mr. Hooker,' he said between clenched teeth. 'I remind you again that Signor Primo and I agreed on a price area several weeks ago.'

Hooker nodded, concealing his enjoyment of the Spaniard's ill-concealed ire. As little more than an observer, he could himself afford a detached coolness that in some measure counteracted the physical high temperature within the room. Marette growled an instruction in his native tongue to the second Frenchman present, and the man leapt up and helped to distribute the brimming mugs of thick, aromatic black coffee.

'I am aware of that,' Hooker replied. 'The difference was fifty thousand dollars between your lowest and highest figures. You are now insisting upon the higher of the two.'

Vega sipped his coffee and scalded his mouth. He banged the mug down hard on the table top, slopping liquid to form a new stain on the wood. 'But I have explained the reason!' he said, his voice rising. But then he glanced quickly around at the bored expressions of the men not involved in the argument, and moderated his tone. 'I was not sure of the quantity I would be in a position to supply. The two prices I quoted Signor Primo took account of the minimum and maximum number of items in the shipment. I am able to let you have the maximum, so is it not right and proper I should be paid the higher figure?'

He looked again at the Italian, and this time received a nod of agreement. Hooker glowered at Primo and was rewarded with a broad grin and an ushering motion of the hands – indicating that as far as he was concerned, the negotiations could stop or continue.

'Not so, *señor*,' Hooker corrected, tasted his coffee and grimaced. 'The shipment was not obtained for our company on order. Your action was speculative. We are offering to take the merchandise off your hands –'

'I have a dozen customers who would be happy to receive the guns!' Vega interrupted heatedly. 'And pay my price without haggling.'

Hooker refused to be provoked. 'As I was saying,' he went on calmly. 'To take the merchandise off your hands quickly and with the minimum of risk to either party. Therefore, in terms of both money and danger of discovery, your overheads in dealing with the company are low.'

Vega opened his mouth to object, but Hooker silenced him with an upraised hand and a cold light behind his pebble grey eyes. 'That apart, it cost you no more to steal X number of guns than if there had only been Y number.'

A short laugh exploded from the Spaniard and he looked imploringly around the table, at everybody except Hooker, '*Señors?*' he exclaimed. 'What logic is this? This shipment is made up of individual items, each of which has as much value as the next. Are not a hundred cans of beans worth more than one can of beans?'

Outside in the bright sunlight, Stark was formulating a plan as he kept listening to the continuing argument within the room, but looked towards the three cars parked in the clearing. Although he had come to this place for the prime purpose of killing Ralph Hooker, his life had taken on a much wider motive since he had been made an outcast. The whole rotten company was his target, whether its representatives spoke English, French, Italian or Urdu. So, as he picked up the threads of what was happening at the meeting in the farmhouse kitchen, he realised he had the opportunity to strike a far greater blow than the death of one man would be.

The Toyota was the car nearest to the window, facing it on a diagonal line. He backed away for a yard or so and then crouched down, running his eye from the level of the sill to the gleaming roof of the car. Then he straightened and checked the angle, deciding that the Toyota would be in the field of vision of the man seated at the range end of the table. He recalled the seating arrangement around the table and pin-pointed the important man as a tough-looking Latin with a bald head and sweat-stained cream shirt. This information availed Stark little except that he could guess this man was not taking part in the bargaining and might therefore kill time by glancing out of the window.

But the possibility was strong enough for Stark to ignore the Toyota and elect to go for the Pontiac – parked further to the right than he would have wished but at least out of sight of the men in the room unless one of them left the table and moved up close to the window.

The decision made, Stark dropped noiselessly down to all fours and crawled across the front of the house, making sure he stayed low enough to be under the window sill. He had to turn sharply at the point where the veranda began. There he stopped, glanced back towards the window and rose into a crouch. The argument within the room was continuing, but only the occasional word was comprehensible to his ears.

'. . . resale . . . you . . . make . . . profit . . . *señor* Hooker . . . cannot . . .'

Stark scuttled away from the veranda and pitched down full length behind the bulk of the big Canadian sports coupé. An owl hooted among the pine trees, an incongruous sound in broad, clear daylight. The crickets complained angrily that their chorus had been interrupted.

'One hundred and seventy-five . . .' Hooker said loudly, but not angrily.

'. . . split . . .' a French accented voice said quizzically.

'The difference . . .'

'I . . . agree . . . Impossible.' This man spoke English with a Spanish accent.

Stark raised himself and peered over the door of the big car. He saw the key in the ignition and his lips curled back in a satisfied smile. He eased open the door and clicked over the key, making the ignition circuit live without firing the engine. The needle of the fuel gauge swung around to show that the tank was three-quarters full.

'Beautiful,' he muttered as he moved to the rear of the car, staying crouched behind the sun-hot bodywork.

The petrol tank filler cap had no lock on it. He began to sweat again as he unscrewed it and set it down on the ground. He shrugged out of his jacket and it didn't help to cool him, but that was not the main purpose. He knelt on the jacket and jerked at the sleeve. The stitches parted with a harsh ripping sound that he was certain must carry to the men in the house. But as he held his breath and waited it was only the insect life of the surrounding countryside which objected to the unnatural noise.

He stuffed the sleeve down through the filler pipe until

only about three inches protruded. It didn't seem enough and he lengthened the visible fuse by a further two inches. It still struck him as dangerously short, but the time-scale had to be cut fine if the plan was to work.

The matches were in a side pocket of his mutilitated jacket. He fished out the book and had to strike three before the material of the torn sleeve lining began to smoulder. Then he waited, mouthing silent obscenities, until a flame licked. It was not strong enough. He leaned close and pursed his lips in a low whistle, sending a stream of air to the seat of the flame. He smelt petrol and fear took an icy grip on his stomach. The flame danced higher and he staggered back on his haunches. Seconds were chipped relentlessly from time. His eyes were fastened on the shimmering flame eating at the material and spitting out charred waste.

'Now!' he told himself. He lunged along the side of the car, jerked open the door and thudded into the driver's seat.

The burst of power from the big V-8 engine was like an explosion across the clearing. He thrust the automatic shift into reverse and stomped on the accelerator. The driving wheels spun, burning ruts in the hard ground and billowing up clouds of dust. Then they gained traction and the big coupé leapt backwards.

Stark hit the brake, wrenched the shift into drive and glanced at the kitchen window. He saw a face as a white blob against the murky interior. Then an abrupt movement. The car roared forward and he spun the wheel, scraping paint on the rear bumper of the Toyota. A puff of white smoke showed at the window. A fraction of a second later the windscreen was inscribed with a star, gleaming in the sunlight. Then the glass became an opaque white mass, like a snowdrift.

His eyes flicked over the rearview mirror and fear re-established a tight grip on his insides. Smoke, much blacker and thicker than from the gun, was swirling across the back window. He smelt petrol again, but decided it was in his mind. He glanced out of the side window and saw the end of the barn furthest from the house. He curled a hand around the door handle, held the accelerator pedal down a second longer, then threw himself sideways: thrusting open the door and diving through towards the rushing ground. The speeding, driverless car exploded with an ear-splitting thud. His body sailing in mid-air, Stark was convinced he was within a split-second of death.

CHAPTER SEVEN

It took Judith Hooker almost an hour to get free of the length of telephone cord which bound her hands behind her back and her ankles to her wrists. She wasted a great deal of this time by attempting to use brute force. But she was not a strong woman and even though the near-hysterical fear for her husband's life injected a greater degree of potency than ever before into her under-used muscles it availed her nothing. Only when exhausted did she search the opulent comfort of the spacious living room for a tool to help her. She found it in the shape of a beaten copper-topped occasional table and the many shards of broken mirror. The glass was in the hearth and the table stood on the fireside rug.

Crossing the room was a painful process, involving a rolling action that placed a lot of strain on her unnaturally positioned arms and legs. But her resolve was strengthened by the image of Stark engaged in a relentless journey of his own. At the edge of the table, where the copper was bent over the wooden top, one of the screws holding it in place had been loosened. A mischievous friend of the twins had done it only that morning, with a screwdriver from a junior tool set Judith had given him for his birthday. Fixing the screw back into place was one of the chores which had awaited her on her return from taking the children to school.

She cut her finger as she scrabbled in the hearth for a suitably sized piece of the shattered mirror. The blood ran warm on her palm as she struggled up on to her folded knees and pushed the razor-sharp triangle of glass up between the copper and the wood. She rested for a moment or two, then began to sway her aching body back and forth, using one gleaming edge of glass to saw through the cord. It seemed to take forever and she began to sob. Her to-and-fro cadence kept time with the spasms which racked her body.

When the length of cord snapped, freeing her wrists from her ankles, she collapsed, pitching full-length to the floor. She screwed her eyes tight shut, fighting for control of herself. When she opened them she was staring at the vandalised piano. Across her mind there flashed an image of the cold viciousness she had seen in Stark's face as he wielded the big hammer, smashing it down upon the notes. She struggled up on to her knees again and began to pump her hands up and down, rubbing the cord against the mirror. There was something close to panic in her actions now and her hands moved from side to side as well as up and down. The keen edge of the glass dug and cut at flesh, but she was unaware of the pain or the sticky warmth of escaping blood.

When the cord parted and she could see her mutilated wrists and palms she viewed them without horror. She was merely angered that the blood greased her fingers so that they continually slipped as she worked at the knots holding her ankles together. But, finally, she was completely free.

When she rose to her feet, she staggered, but righted herself. A mirthless laugh ripped from her throat and she fought against another, recognising the signs of hysteria. She took several steps towards the telephone before she saw the instrument lying on the floor, disconnected. She stared down at her hands, remembering. The sight of the blood frightened her now, but her mind began to function with reason: the flow had diminished to a mere trickle from the deepest lacerations – no artery had been severed.

She stood in the centre of the room, her maturely pretty face cast in an expression which was a mixture of fear and confusion as she recalled the instructions Ralph left her whenever he was away:

'I'm sure there won't be any trouble, Judith, my dear. But if there is, you'll be able to handle it, I know. There won't be any reason to get in touch with the office. They won't know where I am, anyway.'

It had always been that, or a variation: except on Saturday. Before he left in the taxi for the airport, he had added:

'There's a man who has a grudge against the company, dear. We had to dismiss him and he has taken it badly. I can't think that he will come here to Cottonwood. But if he does, Henry will take care of him and see him on his

way. Henry will be staying in the small guest room until I get back.'

Judith caught her breath, recalling another phrase – but this one spoken by Stark, not Ralph:

'Your gardener knows it is.'

She whirled around and launched into a staggering run through the house. In her nervousness, she knocked the key from the back door lock. Her trembling became more severe as she reinserted the key and turned it. She stood on the step, fear-filled eyes searching the partially cut lawn, then coming to rest upon the open doorway of the cedarwood shed at the end of Ralph's greenhouse.

She swallowed hard and moved out of the air-conditioned coolness of the house into the caressing warmth of the afternoon sunlight. Two sparrows squabbled in the branches of an acacia; the scent of new-mown grass rose to set up an uncomfortable tremor in Judith's sinuses; heat shimmered over the spotlessly clean, high polished panes in the greenhouse. As she drew closer to the open doorway of the shed the sights and sounds of the beautiful garden seemed to grow in intensity and a sense of unreality surrounded her. She felt as if she were weightless, drifting in a surrealist dream.

She smelt death without recognising it for what it was. A low insect buzz reached her straining ears and injected reality. She whirled around, seeking the bee: Judith had a near pathological horror of any creature that stung. Then she pinpointed the sound to the shed and had to steel herself to cover the final few feet, forcing one foot in front of the other in heavy slow motion.

She saw Henry. Her scream began as a low groan, then rose rapidly in pitch. The gorging flies rose in a black cloud and she saw it as a deadly massed attack against her body. She swung around, throwing her hands up to cover her face, and broke into a run, channeling every ounce of energy to her pumping legs. The scream rose in a crescendo as she plunged into the house and became a rasping sound deep in her throat as she staggered through the kitchen and out into the hall. She flung open the front door and hurtled down the driveway, unaware that the buzzing sound in her ears was a memory tape in her mind: convinced the black mass, dotted with fiery eyes, was only inches behind her.

She reached the gates and ran through them, the scream becoming a piercing shrillness once more. The driver of the security patrol van saw her as a flash of stockinged legs and red stained hands linked by the vivid green of her dress. He stomped on the brake and wrenched over the wheel, but the woman veered on to a collision course. The bumper hit her legs, violently tilting her body, which thudded against the grille. She bounced forward and crashed against the roadway. The horrified driver spun the van to full lock and one front wheel slithered across the spread blondeness of the unconscious woman's hair, wrenching out several strands by the roots.

Unaware of the aftermath of his visit to Cottonwood, Stark crossed the county boundary of Surrey and Sussex, heading south for the coast. Had he known, he might have suffered a few fleeting seconds of remorse. For his target was the company and everybody who was directly involved in its evil designs. Any innocent bystander who stood in his way was likely to get swatted aside but he had no desire to cause such individuals greater suffering than was necessary to achieve his aims. And he was convinced Judith Hooker was in this category for although she benefited greatly from the operations of the company, Stark was certain she enjoyed her privileges in ignorance of where the money came to pay for them.

However, the period of regret would not have endured for long. Because Judith Hooker was now a part of the past and Stark could not afford to dwell on events which had happened. It used up valuable time which could be better employed planning for the future or taking care of the present. His senseless destruction of the piano had resulted from a bitter memory and had served no useful purpose. Carol's death was no less painful to him and the unleashing of cold rage had not advanced his plans.

Unlike the stealing of the car which was speeding him towards the next phase of his single-handed war against the company. At three-thirty, the need to refill the tank with petrol forced him to halt at an Esso service station. There was a Little Chef cafeteria on one side of the forecourt and he ate a late lunch of hamburgers and coffee before pressing on along the A22, heavy with weekend drivers and their families taking advantage of the first warm day of spring. He turned on to the A26 through Uckfield and in Lewes picked up the sign to Newhaven.

The Channel was blue and calm, brushing against the sand and shingle beach with a motion that was almost apologetic as the tide was funnelled up river. A Dieppe-bound ferry thrashed out to sea, its wash bobbing the small craft moored in the new Cresta Yacht Harbour.

Stark parked at the water's edge and tossed the keys over the side of a dock just for the hell of it. Then he strolled casually among the day-trippers, indistinguishable in his casual clothes. There were several uniformed policemen patrolling the port on foot and in cars, but not in an unusual number. Superintendent Evans, who Stark knew to be leading the search for him, had no reason to expect him to make another attempt to leave the country. He probably thought, Stark decided, that without the help of the company – or a similarly sophisticated organisation – a man marked so drastically by both police and the underworld would not be so foolish as to try such a dangerous move.

But Stark showed no sign that he was risking so much – perhaps even his life – as he made his way into the yacht marina. His intention in heading for a Channel port – he had elected to make it Newhaven simply because this was the closest one to Cottonwood – had been to make use of the company-supplied passport in the name of Michael Hodder and board a scheduled ferry for France. Now he had second thoughts about this. Although the police search for him was obviously not so intensive as it had been immediately after his escape from custody, his description would still be reasonably fresh in the trained minds of immigration men and coppers. And despite his efforts to change his appearance while he hid at the Opal Hotel, he was a long way from satisfied with what had been achieved. Add to this the come-hither look in the eyes of the redhead sitting on the transom of a cabin cruiser – and Stark's second thoughts began to formulate an alternative plan.

'Hi, there, beautiful,' the girl greeted as Stark halted at the edge of the dock. 'Nice day, uh?'

'For what?' he asked.

She giggled. 'For a lot of things.'

He regarded her through the glare-resistant lenses of

the dark glasses. She was about twenty-five, tall and willowy without being skinny. He put her height at five ten and her weight at close to ten stones. There was no flab and she was wearing a bikini to prove it. Her breasts were moderately large, bulging with hidden promise above the token halter top. Her stomach was flat with a few wisps of red down to show she was a big girl now, if extra evidence was needed. Her flaring hips sloping into the well-proportioned columns of her legs suggested a latent strength that would be fun to do battle with.

Her face was not beautiful, nor even pretty. But there was a sultriness about her hazel eyes and a certain arrogance in the set of her full lips that combined with the slightly rugged bone structure of her cheeks, brow and jaw to emanate a blatantly sexual attractiveness. Fully clothed, strap-hanging in a rush hour tube train, she would have presented a challenge to any man with the alertness to give her a second glance. Now, with three-quarters of her tanned, unblemished flesh exposed, she was giving off tacit war cries. And the look in her eyes was a silent bugle call to action.

'Your boat?' he asked, craning his neck to look at the markings on the forward raked transom.

The girl was sitting with her legs dangling, her green painted toenails not quite touching the surface of the water. She nodded, the sunlight setting tiny fires in her thick, shoulder length auburn hair. Then she opened her legs wide. Stark stared carnally at the stretched fabric of the bikini briefs, deciding the down upon her stomach was a false lead to richer pastures. The material clung tightly to the tiny rises and curves of her body, showing she didn't only shave under her arms.

As the adrenalin began to flow, he dropped his gaze and, a moment before the girl closed her legs to obscure the markings, he saw: AMANDA – LONDON.

'You're Amanda?' he asked.

'I don't have much imagination,' she replied, then giggled and added: 'In some respects.'

Stark tore his gaze away from the promise in Amanda's face and surveyed the boat. It was about forty feet long with a sharply raked bow and an area of gleaming polished deck splaying aft towards a low superstructure bristling with electronic scanners and radio antennae. Between the rear of the cabin and the broad transom on which the owner sat was a well with two sets of braces on either side for fishing rods to be attached.

'I'm looking for a boat like this to charter,' he said, returning his attention to her.

She had been studying him closely as he examined the boat, a half smile turning up the corners of her mouth.

'You want to know who my daddy is, beautiful?' she asked.

He shook his head. 'I have to be sure my intentions are serious before I ask a girl about her parents, darling.'

'My daddy's Peregrine Segal.' She waited patiently for a reaction.

Stark's teeth showed in an easy grin beneath the mask of the Polaroids. 'Millionaire property tycoon,' he said.

She nodded, pleased he knew the name. 'Multi-millionaire, actually. Plenty rich enough so his daughter doesn't have to hire out her Christmas present for money.'

Stark clicked his tongue against the back of his teeth. 'So what does she hire it out for?'

'Nothing,' Amanda replied. 'But she likes to share it sometimes. With a friend.'

'You must have lots of those.'

She swung her long legs inboard and stood up. She ran a long-fingered hand through her hair and left it so that a graceful wave hung down to obscure one eye. 'I'm always ready to make new ones, beautiful. Come aboard and have a Campari or something. I don't go for all that navy sun-over-the-yardarm crap.'

'We've got common ground,' Stark said. 'I'm all for satisfying my wants when my wants want satisfying.'

'Take your shoes off first!' she ordered as he prepared to swing off the dock and on to the boat. 'I like things neat, tidy and new looking.' The smile spread across her features again. 'Besides, it's more comfortable without all the silly trappings of civilisation – don't you think?'

'Give me the primitive every time,' Stark replied as he prised off his shoes and dropped down into the well of the boat. 'Except in some cases. This beats a dug-out canoe.'

She glanced over her shoulder at him as she went into the cabin. 'Daddy insists I don't go completely native,' she excused.

Stark brightened his grin. 'Multi-millionaires have to maintain some standards,' he said.

The cabin was divided into two sections by a four feet high wooden partition with a swing gate at the centre. Forward was the wheelhouse, with two swivel seats bolted to the deck in front of an impressive array of instruments. The rear section was furnished as a comfortable compact lounge with well-padded benches on each side, two folding card tables, a drinks cabinet, a TV set fixed to a bulkhead and a glass fronted bookcase crammed with paperbacks.

'You pour the drinks, beautiful,' Amanda said lightly, pushing through the gate and seeming to disappear as if by magic.

Stark crossed to the partition and looked over it. A railed set of carpeted steps went down through the decking of the cabin and he was in time to see the girl's rump sway out of sight into the bowels of the cruiser.

'Campari?' he called.

'That's what I said,' she shouted in reply. 'A lot of it and a little soda. A veritable berg of ice, though. And a big slice of lemon.'

Confident of scoring – and therefore sure he had found a reasonably safe way to get out of the country – Stark poured two drinks, mixing Amanda's in the way she specified and reversing the Campari-soda ingredients for himself.

'Ready!' he yelled after sipping his drink appreciatively.

'And waiting, you bet,' Amanda responded.

The adrenalin began to pump again, the area of greatest activity centred in his loins. 'Darling, you're a dream come true,' he muttered as he pushed open the gate with his hip, both hands occupied with the drinks.

It was easier to go down the steps backwards. At the bottom, he turned, having to keep his head bowed to avoid crashing it against the deckhead. There were double-decker berths on both sides, and a hatchway through a bulkhead into a tiny, well-equipped galley. Sunlight from the ports on the starboard side, facing away from the dock, cut beams through the pleasant murk, holding prisoner a million tiny dust motes. There was little light showing through the quarter opened hatch on the other side of the galley.

'Come on, beautiful,' Amanda called softly, and giggled deliciously. 'You can't get lost on a boat as small as this.'

Stark sipped some more Campari but the sharp bitterness failed to alleviate the dryness in his throat. He crossed the galley and pushed the hatch cover wide. The private cabin had only one berth – but it was a double one. There were two portholes on either side, but gingham checked drape curtains had been pulled across them. Enough dusty sunlight filtered in over Stark's shoulders for him to pick out the main features of the cabin. Of these, the centre-point of interest was Amanda. She was sprawled on the bed, minus the bikini, with only a faint lightening of the skin to indicate where it had once been. Stark's guess about her shaving routine was proved right.

Her body had adopted the pose of a virgin unwilling to submit to the dictates of a reluctant mind – thighs pressed firmly together, forearms against breasts with fingers interlocked. But Amanda's sultry expression emanated a silent advertisement of her desire.

'Pretty native, uh?' she asked.

'Pretty,' he replied, stepping into the cabin.

'Close the door, beautiful.'

'You can call me . . . Mike,' he said. 'I haven't seen enough yet.'

'You will,' she urged.

He closed the door with his heel. Enough light penetrated the curtains for him to see as she unclasped her hands and reached up towards the bedhead. The cabin was suddenly bathed in a green glow from a fixture set flush into the deckhead.

'No, watch!' she said quickly as he made to go towards her.

Slowly, the green deepened into blue.

'And again,' she said with another giggle.

Yellow was next in the automatic colour sequence. Then red . . . orange . . . turquoise . . . finally ultra-violet before green again.

'I can stop it whenever you want,' Amanda said.

'I'm not colour prejudiced,' Stark told her, stepping up to the bed and holding out her drink.

Without the uplift action of the bikini top, her breasts

were not so large as they had looked. But Stark had no complaint as he surveyed them. The dark nipples distended as Amanda received a charge from the mere knowledge that she excited him.

'Take off your glasses, why don't you?' she invited.

He had forgotten he was wearing them. He did as she suggested. The colours from the deckhead fixture intensified.

'And the rest would be nice,' Amanda urged, raising her head to sip at her drink.

The ice rattled coolly against the glass of the tumbler. Stark swallowed his drink at a gulp, but then forced himself to mask his impatience. He succeeded until the final item of his clothing was dropped to the carpeted deck and his anxiety was pointedly displayed.

'You've been eating too much,' she accused, not unkindly. 'But you're still beautiful, beautiful.'

He looked down at the bulge of his stomach which he had actively encouraged during his stay at the Opal Hotel.

'I haven't been getting much exercise lately,' he said, sitting down on the edge of the bed and allowing a hand to rest lightly on her stomach. The flesh was warm and firm: the unshaved hair silky against his palm.

'I'm not making any guarantees, beautiful, but I think I can help. Relax, uh?'

Her free hand fixed a light grip around his wrist and exerted gentle pressure. Stark swung his legs up on to the bed and stretched his length out beside her. She sat up and took a final sip at her drink. Then, with a giggle, she tilted the glass and swung it back and forth between his neck and his thighs. The ice cooled liquid left cold trails up and down his body, but her fingers across the top of the glass kept the cubes from falling out.

'What the hell?' he demanded, starting to sit up.

But she tossed the tumbler to the floor and twisted towards him, silencing him by fastening her full lips to his mouth. With her head and the thrusting cones of her breasts, she urged him gently back on to the pillow, not breaking the kiss until he was fully supine again. Then she hauled herself into a kneeling pose at his side and rested two fingers over his lips.

'Just relax, beautiful,' she whispered. 'I told you I think I can help. I'm going to lick you into shape.'

Her bead bent into the crook of his neck, her tongue darting out to lap up the sticky redness of the spilled Campari. Stark stared up at the perpetually changing colours of the light fixture and surrendered to the ecstasy of Amanda's tongue as she licked greedily at his flesh. Then he screwed his eyes tight shut and arched his body towards her ravenous mouth as she discovered a more delicious taste.

CHAPTER EIGHT

Stark hit the ground with his left shoulder and started to roll. He tucked his head down low and drew up his knees. His forearms protected his face and his hands were clenched into tight fists. His elbows hugged his sides.

The blast from the exploding petrol tank hit him with hot force, lifting him clear of the hard-packed earth and slamming him hard into the side of the barn. The world began to spin with the sun as its pivot, then to pitch and yaw. Every fibre of his body seemed to be stretched and he felt twenty feet tall, aching in every inch. He revised his estimate: he wasn't dead – just a shapeless mass of flesh without a single unbroken bone to give him form.

But when the world stopped behaving like a third-rate ballet dancer on a bad LSD trip, he discovered there was nothing wrong with his vision. Somehow, the Polaroids had stayed in place as he leapt from the car and was blown against the side of the barn. He looked through the dark glass of the lenses and forgot about his own pain.

The car had smashed into the end of the house at the precise moment of the explosion, the force of the blast taking over from the demolished drive. The thrusting metal had been thrown through the neglected woodwork of the wall and now, as Stark watched, the flames of the petrol fire were quickly enlarging the ragged hole.

Stark thought his aim had been good – that the Pontiac had crashed directly against the area of the window. As nearly as he could judge through the dancing flames, a little more than three quarters of the car's length was inside the kitchen. He thought he remembered hearing a burst of shouting just before the tank blew, but he couldn't be sure. He guessed the impact had killed the man at the window, but he had to wait to find out exactly how much damage he had inflicted in terms of human life.

It took no more than fifteen seconds. By that time he had discovered his body was suffering from nothing more than severe bruising: and the fire was racing up and along the façade of the house, the sun-dried timber submitting eagerly to the fierce attack of the flames. Through the frantic crackle of the fire he heard a piercing scream. He straightened his aching limbs and sprawled out flat, dragging the gun from the waistband of his trousers. Heat waves shimmered in the static air of the clearing, but the black and grey smoke of the blaze rose almost straight up with no drift to obscure his view of the doorway.

The stocky Italian was the first to show, tripping over the step at the threshold and pitching headlong off the veranda. Then came a man with his jacket on fire, smoke and flames streaming behind him as he executed a frantic jump. He hit the ground hard and toppled backwards, stiffly like a felled tree. He rolled from side to side, trying to smother the fire. It was Vega, the Spaniard. Hooker and the two Frenchmen fought with each other to get through the front door. Hooker won priority and Marette's bodyguard managed to scramble clear a moment before the flames ate through a heavy beam, dropping a flaming barrier across the exit.

The Spaniard succeeded in smothering the fire at his back and sat up, his face a mask of pain as he carefully slid an arm out of his jacket. Primo stooped to help him as the others looked on in horror, their teeth and the whites of their eyes gleaming against the dark ground of their smoke-smeared faces. Vega screamed as the jacket was eased from his body. Beneath it, his nylon shirt had melted and the flesh of his back was revealed as a blotchy mass of raw tissue pocked with blisters.

Stark viewed the horrific sight dispassionately as he rose shakily to his feet and staggered away from the side of the barn, veering in a half circle to stay clear of the intense heat. It was Marette who recovered first, breaking free of the shock and terror to look frantically around in search of the fire-raiser. But by this time Stark was within five yards of the group. His gait was steadier and the automatic was held in an unwavering aim, ready to zero in on the first man to show a sign of retaliation.

'Maurice!' Marette hissed.

Every man in the group – even the terribly injured Vega – caught the note of warning in the single word and all looked at Marette. They saw the direction of his gaze and swung their eyes towards Stark.

'Stark!' Hooker gasped.

Primo and Marette had heard of him and their shocked

expressions took on a hint of curiosity. Vega decided that a gun could threaten no more pain than he was already suffering and withdrew into his private world of agony, clenching his hands together and beginning to moan through tight clamped teeth.

'*Non!*' Stark shouted as the bodyguard went for a gun in a shoulder holster.

The man looked to Marette for guidance. Marette shrugged, but his smoke-blackened face showed an expression of rebuke. Stark guessed the bodyguard was the only man with a gun and he kept the automatic pointed at him. The man dropped his arms to his sides, looking humble.

'How did you know where to find me?' Hooker demanded, the horror of the blazing kitchen forgotten as a ghastly suspicion gripped him.

Stark swivelled his head, keeping his eyes on the bodyguard but grinning at Hooker. 'You write a neat hand, mate,' he replied. 'But you ought to keep your wife better informed. I had to –'

Hooker prided himself on being able to conceal his emotions in public. But Stark's confirmation of what he had feared ripped away the façade of composure. His body became ramrod stiff, but his hands and the sparse flesh of his face began to tremble. His rage seemed ready to explode with a more devastating effect than the Pontiac's petrol tank.

'If you laid a finger on Judith, I'll . . .'

It was not that he realised the emptiness of a threat in such a situation: simply that he was unable to conceive a punishment severe enough to avenge any harm that had come to his wife. But Enrico Primo was able to consider the circumstances more rationally. He thought that Hooker might lunge for Stark, and extended a restraining arm.

'I left her in a bit of a bind,' Stark admitted. 'No harm done though – except to her dignity.'

'You swine!' Hooker hurled across Primo's extended arm.

The mild expletive was probably as far as Hooker allowed himself to go in the abusive language line, Stark thought. It somehow matched his dignified dress, his elegant bearing and the tasteful luxury of his home. And the whole composite of the man's presence and lifestyle made him more despicable in Stark's biased view. He was so insulated from the muckheap on which he lived he couldn't even smell the stench of it.

'Your move, Stark!' Primo said with a note of confidence in his voice as every man in the clearing heard the sound of a car's engine in high revs. 'You only want to kill Ralph Hooker. The bit with the car took out the wrong man. That was pretty damn clumsy. The gun's better, but if you're going to shoot him, you'll have to kill all of us, too.'

The extended arm ceased to be a barrier between Hooker and Stark and became an indicator, waving around the whole group. The car was drawing closer up the rutted track and Stark had no doubt that it would be one of the Citroens.

'I don't think you'll do that,' Primo added, and now there was something near to a taunt in his voice. 'Only an animal could kill so many men in cold blood.'

The S. & W. 9mm. exploded, the crack of the report sounding almost frail against the dull roar of the fire and the howl of the engine. But the bullet powered deep into the bodyguard's throat, pushing him backwards with blood spouting from the punctured jugular vein. Marette took the second bullet in the heart, his dead body swinging around under the impact before it began to fold. Hooker started to turn, as if he had an idea about outrunning death. The automatic spat lead, once, then again in quick succession. The ejected shell cases seemed to hover in the still air, basking in the sunlight striking them. The first bullet drilled into Hooker's shoulder joint, halting his turn. The second burrowed into his head just below the ear, struck bone and angled up into the brain. Hooker fell across the moaning Vega, bringing a high pitched scream from the Spaniard.

'Aren't I the tiger, mate?' Stark asked Primo as the gun swung to cover the Italian.

'We can do a deal,' Primo pleaded, raising his hands in front of him and taking a step backwards.

'Who are the guns for?' Stark asked, aware that the Citroen would burst into the clearing at any second.

'A group in Beirut.'

'That's a rotten deal,' Stark said. 'Some of my best friends are Jewish.'

He shot Primo in the stomach and as the Italian sat down clutching at the blossoming patch of red an inch above his belt, the Citroen roared out of the pines. Both front doors folded open like wings. Stark ran forward and then dived to the ground beside the crumpled form of the French bodyguard. His hand snaked inside the man's blood-drenched jacket and curled around the butt of a pistol. He jerked it free and glanced at it. It was another automatic – a Colt ·45 Commander. He flicked off the safety catch and looked towards the Citroen as it free-wheeled to a stop.

Sunlight hit the windscreen and bounced away to nowhere. A shot sounded and a fragment of rock-hard earth stung Stark's cheek. He saw feet beneath the open doors of the Citroen, then a head at the side of the one on the right. A shadow fell across him and he snapped a glance upwards. Primo was on his feet, hatred inscribing deep lines across his face. He began to fall, his blood-stained hands splayed in preparation for a strangulation grip. A shot spatted. Primo's knees gave way and he dropped where he stood, his body twisting to show Stark the blood spouting from a ragged hole in the nape of his neck.

Stark rose on to all fours and lunged forward in a sprint start. More dirt was kicked up by a bullet as he dived to the ground in front of the Audi. Two shots sounded close together. Glass shattered and metal crumpled in reaction. Vega continued to hold his position, his agony increasing as the harsh sun blazed on his unprotected burns. He seemed totally ignorant of the dead bodies around him and the deadly bullets whistling through the hot air.

Stark raised himself above the level of the Audi's bonnet and fired the final shot from the S. & W. automatic. He aimed at the Citroen in general and was lucky to hit the front offside tyre in particular. He was answered by two more pistol shots, one piercing the front wing of the Audi, the second thudding into the burning house. He screamed loud to be heard above the roar of the fire, and tossed the empty gun high as he folded his body to the ground, curling up. The discarded automatic clanged on the bonnet and bounced to the ground. The sounds of the fire seemed suddenly much louder in the stillness from every other quarter.

A whispered exchange between the men on each side of the Citroen sounded like the rustle of a small animal scurrying through dried grass. Stark could see the lower half of the car and the feet of one of the men as he peered around the wheel of the Audi. The fat radial interrupted his view of the offside door and the feet of the second man. Two more shots cut across the sound of the fire and Stark pressed himself closer to the hot ground as air hissed from the tyre in front of him and the Audi took on a sudden list, restricting his view still further.

He transferred the Colt Commander from his left to his right hand, first wiping the palm clean of his own sweat and the blood of the dead bodyguard. There was another snatch of low-voiced conversation, then the pair of feet he could see began cautious movement: side-stepping clear of the open door. Stark silently cursed the fact that he could not see the feet of the other man – and the crackling of wood surrendering to the rapacious flames that prevented him hearing footfalls.

But he guessed that both men were advancing on the Audi and then he was convinced of it as the feet and lower legs he could see veered to the side. They intended to arc around the car in a flanking movement and he did not doubt that the moment they could draw a bead on him, more shots would crack across the clearing. Bullets were cheap.

Vega groaned and fell sideways. But he stayed conscious and screamed as the impact triggered a fresh wave of searing pain. Stark rolled clear of the Audi and got an upside-down view of the man who had been obscured until now. The big Colt bucked in his hand. The shot went high and wide, but the man ducked as a reflex action, spoiling his aim. His shot thudded into the deflated tyre. Stark had completed his roll and was stretched out on his stomach. The force of the Colt's recoil had surprised him. Now he clutched the butt in both hands as he sighted along the black top of the barrel. Two fingers squeezed the trigger. The man was less than ten feet away, looking confident as he took aim. The Colt bucked again. The man looked surprised, but unhurt. Then blood bubbled out of his open mouth in a frothing torrent and he was flung backwards. The big forty-five slug tore an enormous exit hole in the top of his head. His brains oozed out to form a glutinous heap on the ground.

Stark jerked over on to his back and sat up. A bullet spat dirt from a spot where his head had been a moment before.

'*Merde!*' the Frenchman hissed.

Stark used the double-handed grip again. He could see only the head and torso of the man above the Audi's bonnet. He aimed for the chest, left of centre. But the gun shot high again, burrowing into the man's left eye. The bullet glanced off the inside of his skull and lost power in the deflection. It did not exit and added its weight to the man's fall.

Stark thought the collapse had set up a vibration in the ground, but the tremors lasted too long. He realised it was his body that was shaking. The big gun slipped from his grasp. He left it where it fell and fought a mental battle with himself, shutting his eyes tight and blocking his ears with his hands to close out the sights and sounds of the death and destruction littering the clearing.

The bout lasted for less than a minute, its end signalled by the sudden stilling of his muscles and the sharp return of pain to many parts of his body. He dropped his hands and opened his eyes. The sight of the six dead bodies and the mutilated flesh of Vega's back aroused no emotion in him. It was the heat of the sun and the fire that raised sweat to his face, armpits and backs of his thighs. His mind worked coolly, detached from the horror now that it was free of delayed fear.

The pain increased as he hauled himself to his feet. He let the gun stay where it had fallen, rested a few moments, then went to where Vega was sprawled, legs and torso formed into two sides of a right-angled triangle. He squatted down and looked into the agonised eyes of the Spaniard.

'You feel so bad you want to die?' he asked easily.

'Nobody wants to die, *señor*,' Vega croaked.

'What's the name of the ship and where will she dock?' Stark asked.

'What will you do if I don't tell you, *señor*?' Every hoarse word seemed to drain away a disproportionate amount of his pitifully low supply of energy.

Stark considered. 'Go down to the café and get some salt. Turn you over on your belly and sprinkle the salt over you until you do tell me.'

'*Si,*' Vega replied. 'A man who has done what you have done, will do anything. The ship is the *El Dorado*. She will berth at Marseilles at midnight unless her captain receives a radio message to alter course for Napoli.'

'One more question.'

'*Si, señor?*'

'You're not a company man?'

'No.'

'Rough luck, mate,' Stark said, standing up, grimacing at the pain the movement caused. 'But if you play around with the company, you ask to get more than your fingers burnt.'

Vega did not understand the comment, but the confusion soon evaporated as he decided it did not matter.

Stark crossed to the Audi and looked inside. He saw the three pieces of luggage with Alitalia tags on the handles. He reached inside and drew out the briefcase with the un-British look. It wasn't even locked. The money was in neat stacks held together by wide bands. It had been tossed in quickly, untidily. Stark eyed it with the same dispassion he had shown towards the bodies of the dead company men. He knew they were dead: he knew the money would add up to two hundred thousand dollars in American currency.

He moved to the Toyota and breathed a sigh of relief that it had been parked in the wrong position to use as a petrol bomb – the keys were not in the ignition. Vega watched him with glazed eyes as he approached, stooped and picked up the remains of the burned jacket. The car keys fell out through the charred fabric of a pocket. They were blackened by soot and Stark wiped them clean with his fingers as he returned to the Japanese saloon. He opened the boot lid and lifted the corner of a piece of sacking. The sample Armalite AR10 rifle gleamed dully with the sheen of oil.

'Is it loaded?' he called as he closed the boot.

'*Si,*' Vega replied. 'In the event somebody wished to test the effectiveness of the weapon.'

'Christ,' Stark muttered as he slid into the trapped heat of the car.

The engine started at the first attempt and he swung

the Toyota around in a tight circle, avoiding the sprawled bodies. The ground floor ceiling of the house collapsed in a shower of sparks as he steered the car on to the track between the pines. The sudden movement billowed black smoke across the clearing, temporarily blotting out the scene. By the time it wafted skywards, Stark had driven around a bend and the pine woods were closed in around him, serene and unruffled.

He wondered why the local fire brigade had not put in an appearance.

CHAPTER NINE

'Miss Amanda, you-all aboard?'

The voice was male, pitched at gravel depth and had roots stretching across the Atlantic to the American southland. Another, more ancient, thread in the tone provided a link with primitive Africa.

'I'd say I was overboard, Roger,' Amanda answered, then lowered her voice to add: 'With happiness.'

She was still naked, but no longer up for offer. The challenge had diminished in the set of her features and her long body was relaxed, sprawled across the bed in innocent repose rather than passionate invitation. The coloured light cycle had been interrupted on green and she had worked a rheostat to dim the bulb. For a long time after she had ceased to writhe against Stark's demanding body, first on top, then beneath, the cabin had seemed like an opaque bubble drifting along just beneath the surface of the sea. But then Stark had introduced reality by getting dressed. The voice from the dock, closely followed by the padding of soft-soled footfalls in the well of the boat, utterly destroyed the sense of detachment from the world beyond the cabin.

Stark had been about to leave the cabin, feeling the need of a strong drink. The girl's sexual prowess was as rich as everything else in her life: her body a soft, pliant machine programmed to give and to receive every variation of sensual pleasure. But the machine was powered by human energy and when her stock was exhausted he was surprised at how much of his own reserves had been drained away in satisfying a demand which at one time he thought was insatiable.

Amanda had seen the approach of his exhaustion and had the presence of mind to curb her panting desire for the animal maleness of him. She had yet to meet a man capable of taking her to the peak of pleasure and when she came across a candidate who showed potential she was always careful at the initial stages of the training programme. There had been too many men in the past whose promise had been dashed by the humiliation of being made aware that they had been unable to take her more than the first stage to the ultimate ecstasy.

For his part, Stark could not have cared less about Amanda's single, first degree orgasm. He knew he had bought himself a boat ride to France and the price he had to pay was not in the least painful. And there was the additional bonus of being without guilt as he rolled free of the sweat-sticky flesh of Amanda's nakedness.

Always in the past when he had thrust himself into a woman's receptiveness, expending lust with no underlying, gentler emotion, there had been a period of remorseful guilt when the coupling was over. But then, Carol had been alive. Sweet, sexually uninventive but unselfishly loving Carol. But now Carol was dead, carelessly and uselessly killed by the company. And although he cherished her memory and was prepared to do everything in his power to avenge her untimely end in any way open to him, he was relieved to discover that unfaithfulness did not demand guilt from beyond the grave.

'Who's Roger?' he demanded of the girl on the bed.

'Not a rival, lover,' she assured him, smiling. 'He's big, strong, handsome and black. He's the captain, or the pilot or the driver or whatever you call a bloke who makes a boat zoom over the waves. It's all right, he won't come down unless he asks first.'

She began to run her hands up and down her body, fingertips trailing lightly over her thighs, downy stomach and then circling the dark crests of her breasts.

'Will he go where I tell him?' Stark asked.

She ceased her self-excitation abruptly and jerked up into a sitting position. Her eyes narrowed and her lips took on a harsh line. 'No he damn well won't!' she snarled. 'This is my damn boat and he'll take it where I damn well want him to take it. You may have screwed me, but don't screw me up by throwing your masculine weight around.'

Stark was surprised by the venom in her tone and the blazing anger in her expression.

'You having trouble below, Miss Amanda?' Roger called from above, a note of concern in his voice.

'Am I?' the girl asked, her voice soft again, but her eyes warning that rage could burst out at the slightest provocation.

Stark forced a grin to his face, but kept his hands behind his back so that she could not see the tight clenching of fists. 'I'm just a male chauvinist pig,' he said lightly. 'Who wants to go to France. It's okay, darling. I'll lay out some bread and travel British Rail.'

Amanda grinned. 'No trouble, Roger. We can leave whenever you're ready.' She flopped out on to her back again and went to work on her nipples with the palms of her hand, rotating them in measured slow motion as she held Stark's half angry gaze. 'It's all right, beautiful,' she assured him. 'Your lucky day. We happen to be going your way – but don't tell H.M. Customs and Excise.' She giggled. 'Of course, where we hit the coast there won't be any fast train connection to Paris or anything like that. Does that bother you?'

'What do you think?' he asked as a powerful diesel engine roared into raucous life.

'I think we ought to have another drink,' she shouted above the noise as the bow of the cruiser began to slap aside the mild waves of the incoming tide. 'To build up our strength for what lies ahead.'

He caught her meaning and relaxed, feeling a faint stirring in his lower stomach.

'Stay up there,' she yelled as he pulled open the hatch. 'We'll get a little sun for awhile first.'

Stark was relieved. His readiness was far retarded from the point to which Amanda's self-stimulation had taken her and he had a faint idea that her attitude to her partners was not entirely one of all-consuming passion. As he went up into the bright sunlight of the partitioned wheelhouse he realised he had been tested. He found it rather amusing, reflecting that he had never before enjoyed an examination so intensely. And the second part would be better still for knowing what was taking place – and the additional knowledge that it mattered not whether he passed with flying colours or flunked.

For the *Amanda* was making easy progress down the estuary and the subdued note of her engines suggested a panting impatience to reach the sparkling blue infinity of the sea, when they would unleash their full power to drive the boat furiously southwards. And Stark's motive for wanting to head in that direction was so strong it would allow nothing to stand in his way, whether it be female and white or male and black.

As the cabin cruiser cleared the estuary and met the swell of the Channel, Superintendent Evan Evans climbed from an unmarked police car halted on the turning circle before Cottonwood and stepped up on to the pillared porch. He pressed the bell push and turned around to survey the sunlit lawns and flowerbeds of the front garden, masking his envy with forced contempt for this exhibition of wealth no honest copper could ever aspire to. He was fifty-eight years old and policeman tall, with the build of a former athlete gone to seed. His face was long and heavily lined, with badly weakened, deep-set black eyes which needed strong lenses in the horn-rimmed spectacles he wore every waking minute. It was an irregular face, the features looking something like a relief map of a mountainous region. By contrast, perhaps in a conscious attempt to compensate for his untidy features, Evans wore his greying hair short and neatly cut. But his clothes complemented his bone structure and skin texture – ill-matching, old and abused by fate and life.

His face, as he turned towards the opening door, re-adjusting his expression to one of legal superiority, was particularly ill-used on this day. A wide length of sticking plaster adhered to the lateral centre of his brow, covering the healing wound sustained when his head had been forced against a wall. And the right lens of his spectacles magnified an angry redness just above his eye, caused by the vicious wielding of a pair of open handcuffs. And his body was host to two other injuries – a broken right arm held across his chest, under his jacket, in a sling; and the unadvertised pain in his groin. All the scars and aches had been unmercifully hammered home by an escaped convict named Stark.

'Yes, can I be of assistance?'

The middle-aged woman had a sour face with skin that looked as starched and as white as the nurse's apron she wore. She held Evans' iron hard stare without a sign of retreat as the detective fumbled clumsily to produce his warrant card.

'Police. It's important I see Mrs. Hooker.'

The nurse glanced at the identification and was unimpressed. 'You are aware that the lady is indisposed?' she demanded.

Evans drew in a deep breath. 'Madam, I am not an ignorant door-to-door salesman. The police force is excellently served by a first-rate communications system. I am therefore fully aware of the facts. I would not be here unless the matter was of prime importance and extremely urgent.'

Evans was quick to lose his temper, but it never broke in the form of an explosion. Those who knew him well quickly recognised the signs as a low fire burning at the back of his eyes and a deepening of his Welsh accent. What inevitably followed was direct action rather than shouted abuse. The nurse knew him not at all, but sensed he should not be trifled with.

'If you'll step inside, I'll go and ask Mrs. Hooker,' she said, standing back to allow him entry to the plush hallway of Cottonwood.

As the nurse moved sternly up the stairs, her uniform apron rustling antiseptically, Evans crossed to the living room doorway and curled his lips in distaste at the wreckage of the piano and mirror. He had known what he would see.

The superintendent had been at his own desk in his regular office when news reached him of Stark's latest assault on persons and property. For after the fugitive had gone to ground and information on his whereabouts had been reduced to a trickle – all of the leads proving false – the powers that be had dictated that the hunt for the wanted man no longer required the full attention of a senior police officer. It was not abandoned, of course. Stark had personally killed several men and others had died as a direct result of his escape, including two policemen. The law never closed the file on an unsolved crime and when the death of its own was concerned, the pressure for a successful conclusion was higher than usual.

But time, and crime, marched on and new villainy raised its ugly head to command Evans' attention. So, although he had discharged himself from hospital against medical advice for the sole purpose of tracking down Stark, the superintendent discovered that the specially equipped office adjacent to the Information Room in New Scotland Yard had been dismantled. And on his return to duty he was re-assigned to his old room and allocated the investigation of an embezzlement case.

As a life-long police officer with a respect for the chain of command, he did as he was told. But, he was forced to admit to himself, he did not bring to the investigation the same degree of concentration and will to succeed that he had shown on the Stark case. For Stark was a very special and particularly painful thorn in Evans' flesh – and not only because of the humiliation and injury he had suffered at the hands of the young man. The prime cause of the superintendent's almost pathological desire to recapture Stark was that the fugitive was a blot on his career. The Danton Electronics payroll robbery was the biggest case Evans had ever handled and it had all the appearances of being easy to solve when he arrested Stark. But the youngster had steadfastly refused to name his accomplices who, Evans was confident, belonged to the underworld organisation known as the company.

So Evans had done everything within his power to ensure Stark received a stiff sentence. He got what he wanted in that matter and was preparing to put Stark through the wringer by a different method when the young villain had broken free. Thus, his continued freedom served to increase Evans' frustration, for retirement was drawing near and he wanted desperately to leave the force with an unbroken record of successful cases. The fact that Stark was apparently intent upon doing what the police had failed at – smashing the company – did not lessen Evans' hatred towards him. Only duly constituted law and order could be allowed to stamp out lawlessness and disorder. The sole alternative was anarchy.

As it happened, when Evans heard about the trouble in exclusive St. George's Hill, the Danton Electronics job was again the only blot on his record. For he had just returned to the Yard after handing over to the Director of Public Prosecutions an airtight set of documented evidence that would ensure a guilty verdict against a smooth operator who had bilked a hidebound insurance company out of fifty-seven thousand pounds.

There were few police officers in the country who were not aware of Evans' hate-based ambition and the men who worked in the same building with him were particularly conscious of it. For it was an unpleasant experience to be in close proximity to the grim-faced Welshman when he was seething inwardly with his self-centred brand of rage.

The telephone was ringing as he entered his office and he snatched it up angrily and barked his name, any satisfaction he felt at the completion of the embezzlement case swamped by the gnawing frustration of not having Stark under lock and key.

A young despatcher in the Information Room spoke to him in high excitement, reporting on a message which had been teletyped to the Yard. The message told the bare facts of the murder of the Hookers' gardener and subsequent accident involving Judith Hooker. The important news was at the end – the delirious woman continually referred to a man named Stark whom she obviously regarded as a threat to her husband.

Evans, feeling some of the despatcher's excitement transferred to himself, first cleared his action with his immediate superior and set the wheels in motion that led to his appearance on the porch at Cottonwood.

'My patient has agreed to see you,' the nurse called down the elegant staircase, her tone making it clear that she was the loser in a recent disagreement. As Evans drew level with her on the landing, she leaned close to whisper: 'Doctor left strict instructions that the patient is not to be excited.'

The nurse's breath seemed to smell of disinfectant. Evans frowned at her.

'I intend to question the lady, not make love to her,' he said stiffly, and went into the bedroom as the nurse gasped her shock.

The room was a big one at the front of the house, bright with sunlight angling in from the late afternoon sky. The furnishings were fragile, the decor soft toned – very feminine. Everything was either white or pink and Evans felt uncomfortable and clumsy. Judith Hooker lay in the exact centre of the big double bed, her slim body hardly raising a mound under the pink quilt. Her wan face matched the paler colour of the room's scheme, except for the dark circles under her eyes and the purple bruise on her forehead. She followed his progress across the room with glazed eyes, the traces of shock still visible through the effects of sedation. She smelled of white spirit and antibiotic ointment. It was an odour with which Evans was unpleasantly familiar.

'May I sit down, Mrs. Hooker?' he asked.

'Please do,' she said in a hushed whisper. 'Have you found Ralph yet?'

There was a Sheraton shield-back chair close to the head of the bed and Evans folded himself into it carefully, fearing it would collapse. It supported his ample frame without a groan.

'No, I'm sorry, madam,' Evans replied. 'It's proving very difficult. His trip abroad apparently has nothing to do with Drake Enterprises. He simply left a message on Friday that he would be away for most of this week. There was no indication of where he intended to go.'

The woman anticipated his next question, and closed her eyes as she said. 'It's useless asking me. Ralph simply said he would be home before the end of the week. I told the other policemen that. He never discussed his work with me.'

Evans could understand that. If Stark had reason to kill Hooker, it could only mean that Hooker was a company man. And – difficult though it was to conceive – there was a possibility that Drake Enterprises was a front for the company. But Evans needed more than mere suspicion to institute a full-scale investigation into such a well-known international organisation as Drake. It was like pointing the finger at Nestlés, Coca Cola or ICI.

But, staggering though the kudos would be for an officer who established such a link, this was a secondary consideration of Evans' visit to Cottonwood. Of prime importance was locating Ralph Hooker: for once Hooker was found alive and well, it would then simply be a matter of waiting and watching for Stark to put in an appearance.

'What about the airport?' Judith Hooker asked suddenly, snapping open her eyes and staring at Evans expectantly. 'The other policeman said –'

'A check is being made, madam,' Evans interrupted. 'And at travel agencies. We know the approximate time your husband's taxi left the house and that narrows it down considerably. But with no idea of his destination, there are a great many passenger lists to go through.'

'You learned nothing from the appointments diary?'

The local police had noted the ragged remains of the

pages torn from Hooker's desk diary in the study and the book had been taken away for a lab test. But there was small hope that an impression had been made on the pages beneath, for Hooker used a felt-tipped pen to make notations – involving very little hand pressure.

'It's still being checked,' Evans told her, then leaned forward slightly. 'Are you absolutely certain your husband gave you no hint of where he was going, Mrs. Hooker?'

The woman injected a trace of spirit into her expression as she met and held Evans' imploring stare. 'Don't you think I've tried?' she demanded. 'Every bone in my body aches and I can't forget what I saw in the shed. But that young maniac is intent upon harming Ralph and I can push everything else but that to the back of my mind. If there had been a single word that might have helped you, I would have remembered. But I can't, so I've given up. All I can do now is lie here and pray the police will find something.'

Her voice began on a loud note and rose with every sentence. She finished the final word as a near scream. The door burst open and the sour-faced nurse stood there, glowering at Evans. Her eyes accused him of a vile crime. Then she swung her attention to the woman in the bed and strode purposefully across the room.

'I'm sorry, madam,' Evans said tightly, unfamiliar with the need to apologise. 'Rest assured we are doing all we can to protect your husband and find the man who did this to you.'

The nurse delved a hand into the bed and eased out Judith Hooker's arm, feeling for a pulse in the wrist. The look she shot in Evans' direction was a tacit command to leave. The superintendent complied, almost walking on his toes in deference to the woman's need for rest. The door bell rang as he reached the foot of the stairs and he answered it a trifle nervously, fearful the nurse had summoned the doctor. But it was his uniformed driver who stood on the porch, his expression animated.

'It just came over the two-way, sir,' he reported. 'The Sussex police have found the stolen MGB, sir.'

Evans immediately forgot his trepidation. 'Where, man?' he demanded.

'Newhaven, sir.'

Evans felt his rising anticipation deflate. It was something, but little enough. If Stark succeeded in getting away from the port by sea, the whole Continent of Europe was open to him. And it had been hard enough to keep track of him in the south of England.

'Back to the Yard,' the superintendent instructed wretchedly as he folded his big frame into the rear of the car, more convinced than ever now that getting a line to Hooker's whereabouts was the best chance of recapturing Stark.

CHAPTER TEN

Roger was an economy size middleweight. He was about five feet eight inches tall, with broad shoulders, narrow waist and powerful looking arms and legs. Stark realised the black man weighed more than he should for his height, but all the excess was solid and he filled his white tee-shirt and faded blue levis in the right places. His skin coloration was light coffee and apart from this the most Negroid feature of the man was his freaked out, crinkled hair. The bone structure of his face had a faintly Latin style, suggesting that his bloodline had at one generation been fed with Caucasian genes.

He had an easy smile and he showed it to Stark with genuine pleasure. It seemed to pinpoint his age in the area of the late twenties. When he was not smiling, Stark guessed that the man would look much older.

'Hi,' he greeted, curling his left hand over his right shoulder. 'Roger Putnam.'

Stark had no hang-ups about colour – only about people in general. He hesitated a moment, then leaned over the gate in the partition to clasp the proffered hand. 'Mike Hodder,' he said. 'When do we hit the beach?'

Putnam dropped the smile and Stark's guess was proved correct. However long he had lived, the black man had packed in a lot of experience, some of it not good. And it was all stored there in his eyes, making him old and wise. 'You better ask the owner, Mike,' he suggested, turning around to face forward, peering through the spray-bubbled windscreen as he replaced both hands on the wheel.

'It's all right, Roger,' Amanda assured, emerging up the stairway. 'Lover boy isn't in any position to cast the first stone.' Her eyes smiled mischievously at Stark. 'Isn't that so, beautiful?'

Stark began to pour the drinks, not looking at the girl in case the extent of his suspicion was visible. He kept his tone at an even pitch. 'Am I supposed to say: what is that supposed to mean, darling?' he asked.

She giggled. 'Don't get uptight about it,' she chided,

obviously catching something despite his effort at concealment. 'You intrigue me, but curiosity isn't one of my strong points. It's just that I think you'd have been perfectly happy to bum a ride in a tin bath with a hankie for a sail if the only alternative was the ferry.'

'Maybe because I'm broke,' he said, turning to hand her the drink.

She shrugged. 'Like I said, I can live without knowing who your grandmother was or whether you copped your first feel behind the school lavs or in the back row of the Odeon. So you're broke – that's okay.'

After the bikini and the nudity, she looked over-dressed. She wore hot pants and a tunic which left her arms and midriff bare. Both were made of wet-look leather which she enjoyed knowing added to her sexuality. She flopped down on one of the padded benches and swung up her long legs, leaving no room for Stark to sit down on that side of the boat. He sat on the opposite side.

'Not until after dark,' she said at length, answering a question he had almost forgotten he asked. 'I already told you we won't be docking at any of the usual places. How does Étretat grab you?'

Stark sipped his drink, visualising a map of northern France. He placed it – a small seaside resort on a bay in the rugged Normandy coastline: closer to Le Havre than Dieppe.

'If it's dark, what difference?' he asked with a shrug.

Amanda nodded. 'That's right, beautiful. It has to be at night. Because the people we meet there won't have an export licence for the watches we're going to pick up. As a matter of fact, they won't even have any papers to show they own the watches.'

He sensed her eyes on him and glanced across the cabin at her, seeing that her denial of interest in his motives was a lie. She was throwing out all the bait she had to try to catch a few titbits in return.

He grinned. 'I'm a mass murderer on the run from the fuzz,' he said.

This time it was a laugh rather than a girlish giggle. Stark glanced across the partition and saw that Putnam was concentrating all his attention on handling the cruiser, which was skimming over the sparkling sea at full power.

'You're not gentle,' Amanda said, pushing a hand down into the neckline of the tunic to caress her bruised breasts. 'But I don't think you're that rough.'

'Just broke?' he suggested.

'That's okay,' she replied. 'I already said that's okay.'

She swung her feet to the deck and stood up, then crossed to the television set and pressed a button. It was a closed circuit set-up, hooked to a videotape machine. As she resumed her relaxed position on the bench he saw where she learned her sexual techniques. The picture was in living colour and there was no soundtrack, because it was unnecessary. It depicted a full-scale orgy, Roman-style. There were a lot of peeled grapes around but few of them were popped into the drooling mouths of the participants.

Stark plucked the glass from Amanda's hand and she returned to reality with a start. Her eyes were shiny with sexual hunger.

'Gets you going, eh?' she asked, the darting tongue now lapping at her lips.

'It's the leather,' Stark told her.

'Not the pictures?'

He tugged gently at her hand and she rose to her feet. 'Why window shop when I've already got the goods?' he asked.

'On the instalment plan?' she said.

'I'm ready to make the next payment,' he told her.

She laughed, and this time it was like a throaty exclamation of physical pleasure. 'Wait until I call you?' she asked.

He released her hand and she banged her knee against the edge of a card table in her hurry to get below. She didn't seem to feel any pain. Stark switched off the television set and looked through a port. The south coast of England was now just a faint dark line between the blue of the sea and the paler shade of the cloudless sky. A line of three coasters steamed along at a sedate pace parallel with the shore. A gull circled overhead, rising on a thermal. The white water from the powerful twist of the cruiser's twin screws sparkled in warm light from the sun dipping towards the western horizon. But not for long.

Within seconds of the *Amanda*'s passing the disturbed water levelled out to merge with the gentle swell and there was nothing to show that the boat had come this way.

'A warning, Mike.'

Stark swung towards the black man at the wheel. But Putnam didn't turn around.

'About what?'

'Have your fun with Miss Amanda. Most guys who get the opportunity usually do.' There was a trace of regret in Putnam's deep-south voice, but not strong enough to imply animosity.

'What's the danger? That we'll burn a hole in the bottom of the boat?'

'Miss Amanda is engaged to be married,' Putnam replied.

Stark kept his tone light. 'So there's no risk of getting caught in the tender trap,' he said and finished his drink.

'Pete Dunlop's a real mean guy, Mike. Like six feet tall and not the beanpole type. Last time he found out about a guy screwing his girl, the guy got cut off in his prime – and I don't mean taken out.'

Stark became tense and stared hard at the mop of freaked-out hair. The black man was still talking, explaining the details of how Amanda's fiancé had castrated his rival with a breadknife. But Stark was not concentrating on what Putnam was saying. 'Taken out' and 'to take out' were expressions peculiar to the company – allegorical terms alluding to death. The fact that the helmsman had used such a phrase cut right across Stark's mood of confidence, that he had shaken free of all chances of pursuit.

He was so deeply involved in thoughts of the ramifications of the black man being a company employee that it was several seconds before he realised Putnam was looking at him with a quizzical frown.

'You said the last time,' Stark asked. 'There were others?'

Putnam returned his attention to the broad vista of empty sea ahead of the speeding boat. 'Three I know about. One did get taken out, but it was an accident. Dunlop likes them to live to regret it.'

'It doesn't bother her?'

The man at the wheel made a sound of disgust deep in

his throat. 'She catches it too, Mike. But he's careful. Not so hard that she doesn't enjoy it.'

'Beautiful, I'm ready!' Amanda called from below.

Stark forced a quiver of nervousness into his tone. 'The bird and me will be parting company on the beach. No chance of meeting him.'

Putnam swung his head to look at Stark. 'Get away fast, Mike,' he urged. 'Who do you think will have the cargo waiting?'

With the man's eyes on him, Stark had to look frightened as well as sound it. 'How will he know?'

'Mike!' Amanda shouted, with a trace of irritation.

Putnam grinned and Stark realised the man was doing him a favour only as a secondary consideration. His prime motive was to give the white man the shakes and spoil his fun with the girl who flaunted her sexuality in front of him without ever laying it on the line for him.

'If you don't make the grade, feller, the broad will need finishing off. And an angry Pete Dunlop with a bull-whip will be the right prescription for what ails her.' He laughed in pure enjoyment. 'But don't let it worry you, Mike,' he urged. 'You got to keep your pecker up.'

Stark almost killed him then. He was on the point of calling to him, jerking the gun from his pocket and allowing Putnam a moment to look down the barrel before squeezing the trigger. But it would have been an emotional reaction, satisfying but stupid. Coolness flooded his brain before he set the impulse into action and he reasoned that although he could probably handle the mechanics of steering the cabin cruiser to France, he knew nothing of navigation. Having left the United Kingdom by the back door, he had no wish to run up against French immigration men.

So, as Amanda called for him again – this time making her impatience very pronounced – he pivoted and started down the stairway. He heard another peal of laughter spill from Putnam's lips as he descended into the cool half light below deck.

Amanda had fixed the light on ultra-violet. The sheets and pillows on the bed, her teeth and the whites of her eyes seemed to glow with a phosphorescence from within. She was naked again, her body spread in readiness on the bed. But she had found some extra pillows from somewhere and had stacked them beneath her buttocks so that her body was arched, thrusting her belly and open thighs invitingly high.

'The accounts office is open, beautiful,' she said.

'I can see it,' he replied, pushing the door shut, subduing the hum of the engine and the thud of the bow against the sea.

She raised a hand and pointed a long finger to the crest of her arched body. 'All you have to pay is lip service for now.'

He nodded and approached the bed. She was breathing fast in anticipation. Then a flicker of annoyance passed over her face as Stark halted and looked down at her head on the pillow.

'No, beautiful,' she instructed. 'The TV's taken care of the preliminaries. You shoot straight at goal.'

It was not Stark's scene and he realised it was a pity Amanda wanted to play the game that way. He was ready, willing and able to match his stamina with her own, but he had to take the dominant role. He didn't think she would agree and guessed that her objections would be vocal.

'With my clothes on?' he asked.

'Drop 'em, like they say at the strip shows,' Amanda ordered.

Stark raised both hands to his belt buckle. Then he flung them down and forward, clasping them together. Amanda's eyes popped wide in startled surprise. The two-handed fist cracked into the side of her jaw. Her eyes snapped shut as her head thudded sideways. The frenetic breathing of sexual anticipation was replaced by a more relaxed rise and fall of her naked breasts. As the tension drained from her muscles, the arch of her body subsided. The pillows slid out from under her.

Stark felt his own aching want diminish as he looked down at her unresponsive nudity. Then, as a sense of bitter-sweet regret threatened to cloud his mind, he launched into a period of frenzied activity. First he found some underwear and street clothes in a locker and dressed her. He discovered that hooks, zippers and buttons were more difficult to fasten than to release. Then he tore a pillow case into strips and tied her wrists and ankles.

He checked that she could breathe comfortably through her nose before he fixed a gag in place.

Then he sat on the edge of the bed and swung the cylinder out of the Magnum. The single brass cartridge left in the gun was an insignificant spot of colour in the circle of dark, empty chambers. He was hit by an idea and he searched the cabin, tipping the contents of the drawers and lockers on to the carpet. All it did was kill time – there was no gun to be found. He made sure that Amanda was still unconscious, then went through into the four berth section. There were two lockers beneath each of the lower bunks and all of them were locked. But a knife taken from a drawer in the galley made short work of three locks. The first two were empty. In the third one was a new shirt still in its wrapper, a pair of slacks, a toothbrush and shaving gear, a colour photograph of Putnam with a good-looking black girl and a Smith and Wesson 9mm Automatic with a fully loaded magazine.

He took the gun back into Amanda's cabin and worked the light sequence until it reached blue. Then he sat down on the bed, slid out the clip from the gun and familiarised himself with the loading and firing actions. After sliding the clip back in, he took a cigarette from a carton he had found during his search of the cabin and lit it. Amanda regained consciousness before the cigarette was half smoked. She groaned, opened her eyes and struggled involuntarily against the bonds holding her hands close together and pressed to the front of her body.

'Just relax, darling,' Stark told her, showing her his teeth in a mirthless grin. 'Enjoy the ride.'

She hated him with her eyes and cursed through the gag, the words emerging as a series of muffled grunts.

'Don't get excited,' he urged softly. 'There's nothing you can do about it. It might have been fun for awhile longer, but you called the wrong shots. Now I've got the edge.'

He drew the automatic from his pocket. It shocked her into silence and immobility for a few seconds, but then she began to struggle and curse again. Stark sighed, took a final draw against the cigarette and stubbed it out against the bulkhead. Then he jabbed the gun forward. The muzzle rammed hard into the centre of the blackened area on the side of her jaw. Her cry of pain was shrill, despite the gag. She stopped struggling and tried to stem the tears from overflowing her eyes. She lost the battle.

Stark used a corner of a sheet to dab the moisture from her cheeks. She didn't fight him and replaced hate with an imploring expression in her damp eyes.

He spoke to her quietly, in a monotone. 'Listen, you're in trouble, but it may not be dead trouble if you forget about having your own way in everything. I'm going to take off the gag – but only so you can talk. If you make any sound louder than my voice is now, I'll ram this gun up the centre of your delight and squeeze the trigger. It won't be fun.'

He made a motion with the gun for her to raise her head and she obeyed. He began to untie the knot of the gag at the nape of her neck.

'Putnam's going to get it sooner or later,' he said. 'I'd rather it be later, but my plans are flexible. So if I have to shoot you, he'll come running and lose a couple of hours of his life. Don't expect any help. This is his gun.'

The strip of material was released and he picked up the automatic again as she spat out the ball of linen which had been forced into her mouth.

'Christ, are you a maniac or something?' she demanded, but remembered to keep her voice low.

'Or something,' he replied. 'Do you know you're working for the company?'

It suddenly became too tiring to hold her head up off the pillow. She let it flop back down. 'What company? I don't work for anybody.'

'So what do you get out of taking your Christmas present on an illegal cross-Channel run?' Stark wanted to know.

'It does somebody a favour,' she answered. 'And it's fun into the bargain.' Her expression became petulant. 'It could have been even more fun – except that you got so uptight about something.'

'How often do you do favours for people?'

'One person.'

Stark shrugged. 'Okay. For Dunlop.'

Amanda pulled a face and stared up at the deckhead. 'Roger's been talking,' she said acidly.

'Not enough,' Stark put in. 'And it wasn't the right time to press for more details.'

'It still isn't the right time – even for me,' she said. 'Because I don't think you'll shoot me.'

Stark sighed and reached down to pick up the ball of linen, damp from her saliva. She shook her head.

'No! This is the third time. What have you got against it? So we smuggle in a few watches? You're not from the police or customs. They don't wave guns around.'

'I'm from me,' Stark told her. 'And I don't just wave them around. Believe me. How do you live?'

She tried to pierce his impassiveness with a stab at humour. 'Pretty well, beautiful.'

'Where does the bread come from? Dunlop?'

There was no lightening of his attitude. Her laugh was harsh, coated with bitterness. 'Peter pays me in kind,' she said. 'I get enormous slices off the Segal loaf. Bread can buy a lot, but it insulates you from a hell of a lot more. You know something?'

'What?'

'I'd never tasted excitement – real excitement – until Peter conned me into using the *Amanda* for a smuggling trip.'

He believed her. The truth of what she was saying was in her voice and in her face. He had expected as much. If Amanda Segal had been anything more than a willing sucker in the company's operations, she would have known better than to allow her personal needs to risk fouling up the trip. Apart from this, there was the fact of Amanda being who she was. A rich father who gave her a luxury cabin cruiser for a Christmas present was unlikely to keep her short of liquid assets. And money was the only incentive for working for the company. So Amanda was in for the kicks. It saved her life. A company employee had to profit by more than enjoyment to be on Stark's kill list.

So he just hit her again, this time chopping at the side of her neck with the heel of his hand when she thought he was going to dab at her cheek. He re-applied the gag and then lit another cigarette. The smoke was invisible against the blue background of the light.

CHAPTER ELEVEN

Peter Dunlop sat behind the wheel of the ancient Bedford truck and finished smoking his fifth Caporal since switching off the complaining engine. He was a big man in both height and girth with a ruggedly handsome face, complemented rather than marred by the two breaks in his nose. He was thirty years old and as he relaxed in the cab of the truck he felt reasonably pleased with what he had achieved in this life span. For, after a false start towards riches on the conventional, lawful road, he had joined the company at the age of twenty and rose steadily up the clearly defined career ladder to his present position of one step below executive status.

And his promotion was in the bag – would follow automatically on his marriage to Amanda. For once a man had proved his capabilities, first in carrying out company operations and then in organising them, it only remained for him to establish his private life on a sound and respectable footing.

So Dunlop had good reason to exude an air of confidence as he watched the waves hit the pebble beach. For neither Ralph Hooker nor Henri Calbiac could boast the ultra-respectability of a wife in the class of Amanda Segal. Amanda's father was a property speculator, it was true, but he gave away as many millions as he kept and when the press was moved to castigate the land wheeler-dealers, Segal was always the exception, held up as an example of how such business should be carried on for the benefit of the mass rather than the individual.

Amanda had her faults, of course, but Dunlop had been able to keep her in line for most of the time. And he had no doubt that, once they were married, he would be able to make his control absolute.

His only problem was in deciding which section of the company should benefit from his executive talents – whether he should work in the United Kingdom under Hooker or in France which was organised by Calbiac. And it was becoming a pressing problem, for as soon as this run was over, he intended to set the date for the marriage.

'There they are, Pete.'

The speaker was a short, pot-bellied man in his forties who was sitting on the running board of the truck, on the opposite side of the cab from Dunlop. As he spoke, he stood up and poked a nail-bitten finger out to sea. Dunlop pushed open the door and jumped down from the truck to peer in the direction indicated. There was a half moon, shedding more silvery light than he would have wished. Enough so that the red and green navigation lights, with the point of flashing blue between them, were hardly necessary as a recognition signal. For as the boat swung to port and showed her profile he was easily able to distinguish the familiar lines of the *Amanda*.

He scanned the flat calm sea to the east and west, then stared out to the north beyond the cabin cruiser. The lights of at least half a dozen ships winked back at him, but all of them were far out in the Channel. He reached back into the cab of the truck and pressed the headlight switch three times. The twin beams of tapering yellow stabbed across the beach, flashing against the white water at the tide line. The navigation and signal lights of the *Amanda* were extinguished and the cruiser altered course again, heading on to a diagonal line which would bring her in to shore close to the parked truck and the waiting men.

The spot chosen to transfer the cargo from truck to boat was a narrow cove bitten out of the spectacular cliffs west of Etretat. The path – it was by no stretch of imagination a road – down to the beach from the N40 route was a series of steep twists and turns marked on maps as impassable to motor vehicles. But the ancient cab and tarpaulin-covered bed of the truck were the only misused components on the Bedford. The chassis and engine, transmission and brakes were in peak condition: the result of the pot-bellied man's loving care in his company owned garage in Rouen. The heavily-laden drive down from the cliff top had been slow but sure. And there would be no problem in grinding back up to the main road again – anyway, there had been none on the two previous occasions the cove had been used for the cargo transfer.

'I start to unload, Pete?'

Dunlop had moved to the rear of the truck and was carefully surveying the hard-packed dirt track and the skyline at the cliff tops on each side of the cove. Nothing moved except the sparse patches of tough grass clinging to pockets of earth in the rock: and this simply bent and straightened lazily under the urging of a gentle salt breeze off the sea.

'I reckon, Louis,' the Englishman allowed at length.

He sounded confident, and he had good reason to be so. For the fix was in with a member of the local *Garde-Côte* and this more or less guaranteed that the gendarmerie would not patrol the area during the vital period. But there was a possibility that something could go wrong and Dunlop was therefore continuously alert for trouble. His cautiousness in all things was one of the reasons why he was so highly regarded by the top men in the company on both sides of the Channel.

The sound of the *Amanda*'s engine, merely ticking over at a quarter speed, reached the beach as Louis untied the thongs holding the tarpaulin flaps at the rear of the truck. He carefully worked out the pins and lowered the tailgate, then swung up. The cabin cruiser's engine was switched off and the boat lost way fast. Water hissed along her hull and there was a soft thud as her bows nudged the beach.

Dunlop went down the slope of the beach in long strides and waited until the boat's stern swung around and she was sideways on to the shore.

'Coming!' Putnam called softly from the well.

A length of line snaked up and out, weighted at one end with a grappling hook. Dunlop picked up the hook and thudded two of the curved points into a huge piece of driftwood half buried in the pebbles. Putnam climbed out of the well and padded forward. He dropped the anchor over the side before the bows were able to swing more than a few feet away from the beach.

'No problems, Roger?' Dunlop asked.

'Not a one, Mr. Peter,' Putnam replied, playing up, as always, the old-fashioned idea of Negroid servility. 'And you?'

'Like well-oiled clockwork. Come ashore and let's get things moving.'

Putnam raised a hand in acknowledgement and leapt from the transom into the knee-deep water at the tide-line.

Like Dunlop and the Frenchman, he was wearing waders.

'Didn't Mandy come across this trip?' Dunlop asked, eyeing the gently bobbing cruiser with disappointment.

Putnam was glad Dunlop had raised the point. He had been looking forward to the confrontation between the organiser of the smuggling run and the unexpected passenger. He had anticipated with relish the prospect of the girl trying to present it as a platonic crossing while the disbelieving Dunlop listened with mounting anger. But it was important that Putnam should not be caught in the backlash of the violent action which was sure to ensue.

So, as the *Amanda* had neared the shore and Putnam had seen the triple flash signal, he had used the wheelhouse-to-cabin intercom to announce the fact. The man had replied with a curt acknowledgement and it was the first sound Putnam had heard since the couple had gone below. But Putnam considered he had done what was necessary to stay on the right side of Amanda. Now Dunlop had himself triggered whatever was to happen next and Putnam could not be accused of stirring the crap.

'She's aboard, Mr. Roger,' he replied. 'With a passenger. I'll go help Louis.'

He spoke his intention quickly, then turned and strode up the beach towards the parked Bedford without giving Dunlop the opportunity to probe for more details.

Crouched in the lounge, out of line with the ports, Stark heard the conversation. The girl was forced into a crouch in front of him, her ankles free of binding but her wrists still tied and the gag held in place. The muzzle of the automatic prodding hard into the nape of her neck warned her against making any muffled sound.

As he heard the black man's rubber-soled boots scuffing against the pebbles, Stark chanced a darting glance through the nearest port. It was only a fleeting glimpse of the tableau on the beach, but it was enough. In the foreground was Dunlop, just stepping into the breaking waves, a hand reaching out to grasp the gunwale of the boat. Behind him, striding purposefully up the beach, was Putnam. He was heading for the dark shape of a parked truck half on and half off the pebbles. There was a small pile of wooden boxes close to the rear of the truck and in the instant Stark's eyes took in the scene, another box was slung to the ground. Stark was struck by the thought that it seemed a rough way to off-load watches.

Then the boat trembled slightly as Dunlop cleared the gunwale and dropped heavily into the well.

'Mandy!' he called.

The girl forced her head around and her eyes were wide with fear as she looked into the impassive face of her captor. Stark forced the girl closer to the decking with a hand hooked over her shoulder. He went lower himself, and rested the barrel of the gun on the top of her head, aiming for the hatchway. Dunlop loomed in the opening and became a frozen shadow as he saw the crouching shapes.

'Come in and keep quiet,' Stark hissed.

Amanda mumbled through her gag. Stark raised the gun a fraction and brought it down hard. The trigger guard hit her skull. The impact hurt, but it was not harsh enough to knock her out. She gave low vent to her pain, then was silent. Stunned by shock, Dunlop obeyed the order mechanically. But before he had taken two paces his brain lost the numbness and worked smoothly at the formation of a plan.

'You crazy or something?' he asked softly, coming to a halt as Stark rose, jerking Amanda up in front of him.

'Mad is a better word,' Stark answered. 'Used as a synonym of anger. You're company, right?'

'If you really thought that, you wouldn't be doing what you are,' Dunlop said, stooping slightly to peer out of a port. He saw that Putnam had reached the truck and was catching the boxes as Louis threw them out.

'Freelance wouldn't dare muscle in on company business, uh?' Stark posed.

Dunlop grinned with his teeth. 'I hear the company has ways of dealing with hi-jackers.'

In addition to the waders, Dunlop was wearing black slacks and a dark blue sports jacket over a black shirt. The knife he could throw like a circus performer was in a sheath strapped to his upper left arm – over the shirt but under the jacket. He raised a hand to scratch his jaw and Stark watched without appearing to be suspicious of the move.

'If I was in the hi-jack game, what would I be snatching?' Stark asked.

'Five thousand Accurist watches,' Dunlop replied easily. 'Very hot. Without the connections you couldn't raise more than a grand on them.'

Dunlop dropped his hand to the left side of his neck and began to scrape his nails over a day's growth of stubble.

'Your friends are handling those cases as though all they hold is cotton wool,' Stark pointed out.

Dunlop shrugged and that allowed him to lower his hand still further without making the move obvious. 'They're very good watches,' he said. 'Shockproof.'

There was quite a lot of light in the cabin – directly from the moon, and glow refracted from the surface of the sea. Stark could see every move Dunlop was making, and every line of his face.

'I'm not a hi-jacker,' Stark said.

'So what are you?' Dunlop asked, spreading his hand wide and massaging his throat, flexing his fingers.

Stark shook his head: *'Who.'*

'So *who* are you?'

'Stark.'

Dunlop's expression said he was company. The name hit him hard and it was as if some physical force dragged down his lids to narrow his eyes and tugged at his lips to twist them into a sneer. Again, for a fraction of a second, his brain went numb. Then there was another instant of time in which he savoured the idea of the company's gratitude for being rid of the man who had proved himself so dangerous to the organisation. Finally he picked his spot – Stark's throat. There was just enough clearance above Amanda's head to miss her and pierce the bastard's jugular vein. He would have to go into a forward lunge and a sideways roll at the instant of release, of course. For Stark would certainly be able to get off a shot.

This entire thought process took less than a second, from the time Stark spoke his name until Dunlop jerked the knife free and sent it spinning. The almost reptilian hiss of the short knife spinning through the air was covered by Dunlop's groan of disappointment and then the roar of the gun's report.

The scratching ploy had not fooled Stark. The moment

Dunlop's hand came clear of his jacket lapel, the blade of the knife flashing wickedly in the moonlight, Stark shoved the girl away from him and fell to the side, squeezing the trigger. As the knife buried itself to the hilt in the padded back of the bench seat, the 9mm. bullet blew a hole in the centre of Dunlop's forehead. It went through the bone cleanly, the impact slowing it. But not enough that the soft nose failed to probe into the goo of the brain. Blood fountained out until the nervous system signalled death and the heart ceased to pump. Dunlop twitched and became still. Cordite was strong and acrid in the cabin. The pollution thickened as Stark jerked the Magnum from his pocket and pumped its last bullet into the unresponsive flesh of Dunlop's back. A black hole appeared in the jacket material, but there was no blood.

He had not shot a dead man for the hell of it. As muffled sobs fought through Amanda's gag, Stark glanced out of the port. He saw Putnam swing around to look towards the boat as Louis jumped from the rear of the truck. He ducked back and stooped, pressing his lips close to the girl's ear as he worked on the knot holding the gag in place.

'Your line is: 'Roger, they've shot each other. Hurry.' His voice was a rasp, and the girl tried to pull her head out from under his face. 'If you were really hung up on him, fluff your line. You'll be able to marry in that big cathedral in the sky.'

The strip of linen parted and she spat out the ball of material with a violent sob.

'Say it loud!' Stark ordered, jerking her into a sitting position. 'No need to act.'

She turned her dead white face towards him and saw that he would shoot her without a moment's hesitation. It was in every line, every curve, every indentation of his granite-like features.

'Roger,' she said, and it was just a hoarse whisper. The muzzle of the automatic rammed hard into her hip. 'Roger!' she screamed. 'They've shot each other. Come quickly, please!'

He had been right. Terror rang in every word, the tone balancing on a thin line between a shout and a scream.

'You're a director's delight, darling,' Stark told her, rising slightly to peer out through a port.

The two men were pounding down the beach towards the boat, Putnam moving like an athlete who had been training for this very occasion. Louis lumbered along in the wake of the black man, wavering from side to side, out of breath from exertion before he began to answer the high-pitched plea.

Stark let go of Amanda and moved on all fours to the hatchway. There, he stood up and waited. When running feet splashed into the breaking waves he stepped out into the well of the boat. Putnam halted abruptly, both hands curled over the gunwale to assist his leap aboard. His eyes and teeth showed up very white against his black skin.

'Dunlop wasn't good,' Stark said softly. 'But he wasn't lousy. You're fast, but you ran the wrong way.'

Putnam tried to duck below the cover of the boat's hull. Stark aimed for his chest. The bullet spiralled into the black man's right eye and he was flipped over backwards into the waves, his scream high, thin and short. The edge of the sea accepted his body gladly and tried to suck it out into the depths. It almost succeeded, the head and torso sliding under the keel of the boat as she rose on an incoming wave. But then the *Amanda* subsided into a trough. The dead man's stomach burst open like a rotten orange under a hammer blow. Blood-streaming entrails wafted in the dark water. The keel rose and fell again. Putnam's back bone snapped but the flesh of his back remained intact. The sea renewed its claim and the boat acceded. The body, almost torn in half, was sucked away by the stained water.

On the beach, Louis saw Putnam go down and tried to halt and turn. But his momentum was too great on the slope of the pebbles and he stumbled. He flailed his arms in an effort to regain his balance. But he went headlong, his skull cracking hard against the pebbles. Stark lunged to the side of the boat and tried to draw a bead on the tumbling form. Louis flipped head-over-heels again and screamed as he came to an abrupt halt. The sound died and he lay absolutely still, his obese body arched across a piece of driftwood.

Stark vaulted over the side into the waves and kept the gun aimed as he neared the motionless form. Louis's eyes were open and there was blood on his lips. Stark tipped him over on to his face, using the toe of his shoe. Two spikes of the grappling hook had pierced the Frenchman's back. Blood emptied from the dead mouth. Stark guessed at least one of the points had reached a lung.

'Help me, please?'

Stark turned towards the boat. The girl for which it was named was standing in the well, swaying with the motion of the deck beneath her feet. Her face was like a splash of white luminous paint against the silvery blackness of the moonlit sea behind her. The strips of linen holding her arms tight to the front of her body looked almost dark in comparison.

Stark ignored her for as long as it took him to glance to left, right and behind him. The towering ruggedness of the high cliff faces added volume to each sound within the cove, but would trap the waves, ensuring the noise did not carry beyond the area. But it wasn't a place to waste time in.

He had the alternatives of truck and boat and decided it had to be the former. The boat offered the most direct escape route, but once clear of the cove he would have to look for another isolated landing place and that was risky. He was already safely on French soil, with a means of transport ready and waiting.

The decision made, he crunched down to the tide line and splashed into the water. He surveyed the girl stoically.

'Are you . . . are you going to kill me, too?' she asked. Misery and resignation fused in her expression.

'Turn around,' Stark told her.

'I'd rather see you do it,' she challenged. Her body was trembling, but she managed to inject some strength into her tone.

'Don't be stupid,' Stark said, and pushed the automatic into his pocket.

A glimmer of hope started a minor fire behind her eyes. She did as she was told. He leaned across the gunwale and untied the knots. He told her to face him again, then to hold out her hands. She complied and he unfastened her final bond. He noticed that Amanda had not been drained of all her spirit. While moving from the cabin out into the well of the boat, she had managed to bring the discarded Magnum with her. It rested at her feet.

'Can you handle the boat?' he asked, waiting for her to make a try for the gun.

'I wouldn't know which switch worked the windscreen wipers,' she replied. Instead of the Magnum, it was the body of Dunlop which held her attention, sprawled across the cabin decking. 'I knew he liked knives. I didn't know he was that good with them, though.'

'Come with me,' Stark invited, holding out a hand.

Now she glanced down at her feet, but it was too open to be the prelude to an aggressive act. Stark waited.

'I was going to kill you,' she said simply.

Stark shook his head. 'Not with that, darling. It's empty.'

She accepted the comment without reaction, then took his hand to help her over the side. She quivered at the chillness of the water. She tried to walk up the slope of the beach unsupported, but after a few yards had to hold on to his arm. They reached the rear of the truck, where about twenty-five or thirty boxes were heaped. She watched in silence as Stark used the butt of the automatic to knock the top off one of them. When the wood splintered and he rose, holding the box out towards her, she gave a gasp of surprise.

'Not watches?'

Inside the box was a clear polythene bag, tightly packed with white powder. He used the muzzle of the gun to burst a hole through the plastic. He licked his index finger, probed the hole and touched his tongue to the coating of fine grains.

'Not watches,' he agreed wryly. 'I'm no expert on this stuff, but I'd guess heroin. Already cut with milk sugar.'

'Jesus Christ! The bastard!' Amanda snarled.

If Stark had not already decided the girl was a more or less innocent sucker, this exclamation and the expression which accompanied it would have convinced him. She was a girl out for kicks, but drew a very clear demarcation line to show where the fun had to stop. Stark looked into the rear of the truck. There were still three more boxes to off-load, but they had been moved to the tailgate. He dragged them clear and dropped them to the ground.

'Did he know you had a thing about narcotics?' Stark asked the girl.

Amanda was staring down the beach at the boat, her

expression suggesting she wished Dunlop would spring to life so she could kill him herself. 'You know what he said?' she asked, and didn't wait for an answer to the rhetorical question. 'He said it would be a gas to bring in some watches for a friend of his. He said that even if we got busted by the fuzz, daddy had enough pull to square it. My God, if daddy knew I was mixed up in this, he'd lock the cell door himself and throw away the key. My young brother's in a wheelchair because he thought he could stop a car with his bare hands at the top of an LSD trip.'

'Rough,' Stark said simply, moving to the cab and swinging up behind the wheel.'

She ran to him and reached out to stop him closing the door. 'Take me with you, please?' she implored.

'That's your boat down there,' he pointed out. 'They'll make the connection.'

She shook her head. 'I don't care. Take me with you. I want to get away. I don't care where.'

He looked down at her face, no longer sensual: almost childlike in the pathetic plea of its expression. 'Can you speak French?' he asked.

'I was educated at the Sorbonne,' she replied, a note of excitement entering her voice. 'I'm told I don't even have an accent.'

Stark nodded and leaned across to spring open the other door. 'You've got yourself a ride,' he said after waiting for her to climb up into the passenger seat. 'You can try out your fluency with an anonymous tip-off to the local fuzz.'

'About all this?' she asked as he started the engine and jiggled the gear stick into reverse.

'Most of it,' he replied after he had turned the Bedford around and spotted the start of the track in the headlight beams. 'You can leave out my name.'

Amanda found it in herself to paste a wan smile on her face. 'Modest, as well,' she said as the engine note changed, straining powerfully against the drag of the first incline.

CHAPTER TWELVE

Stark's love affair with cars had once led him into a job ferrying vehicles to their new owners. For the most part the trips had been confined to the United Kingdom, but there had been an occasional trans-European journey. Thus, when he had negotiated the twisting steepness of the track to the top of the cliffs and saw the name Rouen on a directional sign, he recognised it from the past.

At first the route was by way of narrow side lanes, but then he found the N13 priority road and he was able to barrel the five-tonner along at its maximum speed for most of the way to the Prefecture of the Seine-Maritime department. It was just short of eleven o'clock when he swung the Bedford on to the forecourt of a Gulf service station at the northern edge of the town. He told Amanda to ask the attendant to fill up the thirsty tank.

Then he took her into a café across the street. Their clothes had dried out from splashing in the waves at the cove and Amanda had used some of the time during the silent ride to apply make-up to her pale face. The only visible mark of her experience was the bruise on her jaw, which had taken on a yellow tinge. As they entered the café, a quarter-filled with men and a few women mostly watching a football game on television, they attracted only the mild curiosity which strangers expected to draw.

Stark ordered two coffees and cognacs and a *jeton* from a bartender who understood his French without difficulty. They carried their own drinks to a table at the opposite end of the room from the TV set. The other patrons lost interest in them as the football match produced a disputed goal.

He eyed Amanda suspiciously, expecting to see her snatch up the brandy and suck at it ravenously. But it was the coffee she tried first, chasing it decorously with a sip of cognac. After her venomous outburst on the beach, she had maintained a stony silence and Stark had wondered if she had been making an effort to contain the shock within her – at risk of a dangerous explosion later. But as he looked at her in the dim café lighting, she appeared as composed as when he had first seen her lounging on the transom of her boat.

'Don't worry,' she said, looking up suddenly and meeting his searching gaze. 'I'm not the kind of female who throws a fit when something blows a hole in her nice secure world.'

'It's a big hole,' he pointed out.

She shrugged. 'Pete was fun while he lasted. I would never have married him, you know. But if you hadn't shown him up for what he really was, I suppose I would have cried for him.' She picked up the small brandy balloon and stared into the amber liquid it contained. 'Even now, maybe, there'll be lonely nights when I'll remember the good times and make my pillow wet.' She returned her gaze to the man across the table from her. 'It will help if I can stay with you for awhile.'

'For what?' Stark asked.

She smiled. 'I've got an idea you can be fun when you don't have a gun in your pocket.'

'I'll always have a gun in my pocket, darling,' he told her.

'All right,' she allowed. 'In your hand, then.'

There was a quiver in her voice now, and she quickly lifted her glass and swallowed the warmth of brandy. Stark recognised the signs of fear and realised her self-assurance was not so strong as he had thought. He pushed her a little more. 'I'm no rich girl's stud,' he said.

She sucked on the knuckle of her right index finger. 'You can call the shots,' she told him, and started at the unfortunate choice of phrase.

Stark nodded. 'Okay. You can come along for the ride. For as long as you're useful to me.' He slid the *jeton* across the plastic table top. 'Call the fuzz and tell them there are three bodies and a heap of heroin on the beach somewhere near Entretat. That's all. Keep it short and sweet.'

She picked up the telephone disc. 'Aren't you coming to check I don't say anything out of turn?'

He showed his teeth in a grin. 'I'm the trusting type,' he answered. 'Just as you'll have to trust me when I promise not to make a run for the truck while you're talking to the law.'

She considered the deal for a moment, then nodded and stood up. The televised football match had hit a dull patch. Some of the male viewers eyed Amanda's willowy frame lasciviously as she moved to the wall telephone and began to make the call. The cognac suffused Stark's belly with a warmer glow than usual and he showed a carnal expression of his own as he watched the girl. But then she got her connection and he raised his eyes away from the curves of her body to the bruised profile of her face.

Her jaw moved rapidly and continuously for ten seconds, allowing no time for the man at the other end of the line to interrupt. Then she slammed the handset down on the cradle and swung around to stride hurriedly back to the table.

'What did they say?' he asked as he got to his feet.

She smiled. '*Bonsoir*. Then a few bits of words.'

Stark nodded. 'Let's go.'

'*Bonsoir!*' the bartender called.

Amanda replied, backing it with a smile the man would be able to take to bed with him and use as the basis of an erotic dream. The girl was still looking over her shoulder at the grateful bartender as she followed Stark through the doorway. So, when Stark pulled up short, she crashed into him.

'Be useful again, darling,' he hissed, without turning towards her.

She followed the direction of his gaze and saw the caped gendarme in the act of lowering himself to the cobbled street after peering into the rear of the Bedford. The girl's smile faded fast, but she renovated it in an instant as the uniformed policeman swung towards the café doorway.

'*Est-ce votre camion, monsieur?*' he wanted to know.

Stark understood the question, but the suspicious expression on the cop's face warned him against a direct answer. Amanda overcame her surprise quickly and stepped forward, shooting rapid-fire French at the gendarme. He was a bulky man in middle years with a cast in his right eye. Stark guessed he was fully aware that the girl was turning on the charm for her own ends: but his attitude melted away. Stark listened carefully, endeavouring to nod or shake his head in the right places as he translated the occasional word or phrase.

Finally, the cop opened the passenger door of the Bedford and helped Amanda to climb up into the seat. He continued to hold the door wide, his good eye drinking in the sight of Amanda's casually exposed thighs until Stark climbed behind the wheel. Then he gave a cheerful wave and Stark grated the gears in his haste to set the truck rolling.

'Did I do all right?' Amanda asked proudly, wriggling in the seat and tugging down her skirt to a more modest level.

'Was he just being nosy?' Stark asked, glancing into the rearview mirror and catching a glimpse of the cop as he entered the café.

'The front tyre on your side is almost bald of tread,' Amanda replied. 'He was just acting like a copper by peeking in the back. I told him we only had a short way to go and that you would change the wheel in the morning.'

'It took you a lot of time to exchange that amount of information,' Stark said as he negotiated the town centre and followed a sign for the autoroute to Paris.

'There was a slight problem,' she admitted.

'So don't do all the worrying yourself, darling,' Stark snapped. 'Share the burden.'

'The Frenchman who was killed on the beach was named Louis Blanchard.' She had moderated her tone in the face of Stark's irritability. 'He runs a garage in Rouen. The copper thought Blanchard owned this lorry. I told him we borrowed it from Blanchard.'

'Christ!' Stark muttered, as he passed a de-restriction sign and pressed the accelerator to the floor.

He glanced at the girl and saw that, despite the compromise of her tone of voice, the conversation with the gendarme had not worried her. For the corners of her mouth were turned up in a gentle smile – and her eyes gleamed to reveal the full extent of her enjoyment. She knew exactly what the cop's knowledge meant and it only added a new force of exhilaration to the biggest fun-kick she had been on for a long time.

Stark drove hard down the N13 and joined the Paris-bound lane of the A13 autoroute at Louviers, his mind busy with weighing the advantages of Amanda's command of French against his conviction that the girl was more than a trifle unbalanced.

In a troubled world, he was not the only man with an unresolved problem. Back across the Channel, a light glowed in the face of a towering office block on the Euston

Road. It gleamed like a pathetic distress signal from a tenth floor window in the Drake Enterprises Building. Behind the window was a spacious office, its oak panelled walls and heavy ornate mahogany furniture an oasis of nostalgia in the laminate and stainless steel design of the rest of the building. Gold blocked lettering on the outside of the door proclaimed that the office was the sanctum of RALPH HOOKER – CHAIRMAN. But the sallow-faced, expensively-suited, middle-aged man hunched at the big desk was not the head of the United Kingdom branch of the company hiding behind the cloak of Drake Enterprises.

His name was Hugh Nairn and to every other employee of the front organisation he was known as the personal assistant to the chairman. In fact, he was second only to Hooker in the chain of command that secretively linked this ultra-respectable office to countless underworld operations throughout the United Kingdom.

With Hooker out of the country, Brian had authority to pick up one of the three telephones on the leather-topped desk and order anything from a raid on a second-hand furniture shop to the death of anybody who threatened the company.

Indeed, he had already made one such call today: shortly after Superintendent Evans had left at the end of an interview filled with sly innuendos about a possible investigation of Drake Enterprises. This call was to Colby Cabs, the London-based division of the company which took care of the strong-arm jobs. The call was not to instruct that Stark should be taken out, of course. Nobody on the company payroll could be in any doubt that the vicious renegade was to be killed on sight. So Nairn had talked with Jake Colby personally, reporting that Stark had broken cover and instructing that the campaign to take him out should be stepped up. There had been no need to impress urgency on Colby. The very fact that Stark had struck at the home of the big man was sufficient to let Colby know that the bastard was top priority again.

Thus, Nairn had done what he could at this end and he was clear in that department. His late night dilemma was concerned with whether or not to put Hooker in the picture. Under normal circumstances, Nairn's brief was crystal clear. Whenever Hooker was out of the country on company business, his second-in-command was to take charge of United Kingdom operations and make all decisions on his own initiative. Hooker left the country only on business which the international board considered of foremost importance. In such situations, therefore, Hooker did not want to be involved with other problems.

But this was by no means a normal circumstance. Stark had calmly gone to Cottonwood, killed a bodyguard and subjected Judith Hooker to a terrifying experience. And there was the slim possibility – Nairn found this hard to credit – that Stark had learned of Hooker's movements in Europe. This was information which even Nairn did not possess. He had an idea his boss was in Milan, but that was pure conjecture. And he had a telephone number in that city – one which he was not supposed to have.

To call that number might fetch Hooker racing home, filled with gratitude for Nairn's action. On the other hand, it could interrupt delicate negotiations and lead to Nairn's strength of character being questioned at international level.

So it was that, as a case clock on the mantelshelf of the faked fireplace struck midnight, Nairn switched off the office lights and went out into the corridor. As he rode down in the lift and then drove his Rover three-and-a-half litre out of the basement garage, he fought an inner struggle with himself against admitting the factor which influenced his decision. But then he realised the foolishness of such a conflict. He was in the air-conditioned privacy of his car, and there was nobody to witness any physical revelation of his feelings. So he allowed a small smile to brighten his sallow features, contemplating the distinction of the chairmanship for himself if Stark succeeded in taking out Ralph Hooker. And what if that didn't happen? The smile faded for only a few moments for, as Hooker would have to realise, Nairn had done nothing but follow the rules laid down by the big man himself.

CHAPTER THIRTEEN

In the small hours of Monday morning, with a fine grey mist rolling across the rich green pastures and sleeping towns and villages of the Loire Valley, Stark roused the dozing Amanda as he halted the Bedford in a side street of Fontainebleau. She had drifted into sleep as the truck by-passed Paris to the west. Now she blinked and stretched, orientating herself with casual ease to the strangeness of her environment. While sleeping, she had occasionally murmured and moaned, but it was obvious her imagination had not stirred up the horrors of the cove from the depths of sub-conscious. And now, as she peered through the windscreen across the roofs of a line of parked cars, there was nothing in her voice or expression to suggest she had any regrets over what had happened or her course of action since.

'Where are we?' she asked, stretching out the final word with a yawn.

'Fontainebleau,' he told her.

'Destination?' she asked.

He shook his head. 'This heap's got one of the sweetest engines I've ever heard, but it loses its punch at a hundred.'

Her eyes widened. 'Miles an hour, for Christ's sake?'

'Kilometres,' he corrected, pushing open the door. 'Stay here until I find us a new set of wheels.'

She watched him as he approached the car parked immediately in front of the Bedford and saw him try the driver's door without success. She found some cigarettes under the dashboard and hunted for matches. There were not any there. She sighed and looked along the street, meagrely lit by four overhead lights haloed by mist. On one side was the long bulk of a factory, with a fading sign on the roof to advertise it was the home of a furniture manufacturer. Shops lined the opposite pavement, with two-storey flats above. None of the windows was lighted. She recalled visiting Fontainebleau on a number of occasions when she had been studying in Paris, but she had never been in this quarter. It depressed her to survey the bleak, early hours vista through the windscreen, especially when compared with those days away from university. Then she had been in the company of one or other swinging student – getting drunk in a bar close to the palace before barrelling out into the forest and screwing in the back seat of her little Fiat Eight-Fifty.

A soft whistle interrupted her train of thought and she focussed on Stark, waving to her from half a dozen cars along the street. And immediately her depression was lifted. He was no over-anxious kid with sweaty hands and a surfeit of anticipation to ruin his performance. He wasn't any superman, either. But he was the best she had possessed in a long time and he might just be able to deliver the complete goods if she handled him right. And it would have to be right. So she hoped that her suddenly aroused excitement did not show as she approached him. Her nipples ached as they pressed against the restriction of the bra, and the quivers running through her inner thighs threatened to set her whole body trembling. But she fought to control herself.

Stark had both doors of a pale blue Mustang wide open and had ducked under the raised bonnet as soon as he saw her leave the truck. He was in no mood to cope with an oversexed girl reaching for the pitch of heat. She slid into the passenger seat, making sure her skirt was pulled down to its fullest extent. The engine burst into life as two wires were crossed. Amanda screwed her eyes tight shut and gave herself a mental tongue-lashing. The bonnet crunched closed and Stark sank into the seat behind the wheel. She was certain she could smell the maleness of him, but when she cracked her eyes to peek at him, his profile was set in a hard line of grim satisfaction.

'You can sleep for another hour, darling,' he told her flatly. 'Then it'll be your turn to drive.'

He checked the rearview mirror just before he turned out of the side street. The windows stared down blindly upon the vacant parking space left by the Mustang.

'Aren't we going to stop anywhere?' Amanda asked, a trifle irritably despite her good intentions.

'Sure we are,' Stark told her.

She brightened instantly. 'Where?'

He kept her in suspense, concentrating on his driving until the Mustang came clear of the town and gave a throaty roar of released power in reaction to the demanding pressure of his right foot.

'Nice,' he said, flashing her a knowing grin. 'You think you can keep things on the boil until then?'

'You'd be an easy man to hate,' she shot back, and the thin veneer of a forced smile did not quite conceal that she meant what she said.

He stared ahead, at the black ribbon of road which seemed to be being reeled in by the thrusting front end of the car. 'It adds to the charge you're getting out of all this,' he pointed out, making it a statement rather than a question.

'Screw you!' she flung at him and wriggled down into the seat of the car. 'You're so damn smart, aren't you?'

She closed her eyes and tried to shut him out of her mind. She used the technique of recalling the fear and horror of the boat ride and the beach. But it was not successful. Stark was absolutely right. The fact that he was a cold-blooded killer – more: that he had almost killed her and she had actually seen him shoot down two men – honed her anticipation of sleeping with him to a nerve-jangling keenness.

Anticipation of a far different type had a strong grip upon the mind of Superintendent Evan Evans as the Britten-Norman Islander lost height over the Seine estuary on a glide path into Deauville airport.

The pilot made a perfect three-point landing and followed the ground controller's instructions to taxi to an area left of the terminal complex. Two men climbed out of a black Peugeot saloon and held their hats against the swirling air from the spinning propellers of the three engines. Then the power was cut and the co-pilot moved into the cabin to push open the door and drop the steps. The men on the ground moved forward.

Both were of medium height, in their early forties and were clean shaven. The one with a mole on the right side of his chin introduced himself as Chief-Inspector Manet and the man with him as Inspector Bergeret. Evans knew them both to be members of the Paris Sûreté Nationale drug squad on temporary attachment to Interpol. Evans had no French, but Manet spoke excellent English, his partner none.

The night had been clear when Evans left Lydd airport,

but the Channel developed heavy cloud cover a few miles out and a few spots of cold rain spat at the men before they were able to get into the unmarked police car. Bergeret drove, with Evans and Manet in the rear.

'Anything new?' Evans asked, adjusting his cradled arm into a position which gave him least pain.

'We have traced them to Rouen, superintendent,' the French police officer answered. 'Perhaps one hundred kilometres from the cove where they landed. It was police headquarters there which received the tip-off and a local call was suspected. We now know that Stark and Miss Segal were in the town at the time the tip-off was given. We feel it is safe to assume that the girl herself made the call.'

The chief-inspector went on to explain how the patrolling *agent* had checked over the Bedford truck and questioned the couple about its ownership. But he had no reason to be suspicious of the girl's explanation and did not even report the incident until he learned of the violent end of Louis Blanchard.

Evans nodded his acknowledgement of the additional information, disappointed that the trail of the fugitives had gone cold at such an early stage. It had the feel of being very hot indeed when he had been roused from his bed in the modest semi-detached house in Staines and snatched the receiver off the cradle. He barked his name into the mouthpiece, expecting to hear the voice of his night duty deputy relaying the news that Ralph Hooker's destination had been revealed.

But it was the rounded tones of Assistant Commissioner James which penetrated the hum and static of the wire. The Interpol Section of New Scotland Yard had received an account of the mêlée in a cove on the Normandy coast and the cabin cruiser named *Amanda* provided a link with Newhaven, where Stark had abandoned the stolen MGB on the quayside. It was an odds-on chance that Stark had played a large part in the shooting, especially since it bore his trademark of a tip-off so that the police could pick up the pieces of his violence.

The French police had requested the assistance of a British officer and Evans was the obvious choice. Arrangements had been made for him to be picked up by a car from the local station and driven to Lydd Airport where a specially chartered aircraft would be waiting to fly him across the Channel.

In response to a question from Evans, the assistant commissioner said that Ralph Hooker's name did not appear on any passenger list for flights out of Heathrow on Saturday. A check was being made on likely aliases, but even if this proved affirmative – meaning a forged passport was used if Hooker had left the country – there would be no investigation of Drake Enterprises unless and until Hooker was questioned and admitted to criminal dealings. Even then, James insisted, it was unlikely that Drake would be subjected to official inquiries. It was inconceivable that such a company could have criminal tie-ups. Why, Mrs. James was an ordinary shareholder, the dividends she received being paid over twice yearly to the parish church restoration fund.

Evans used one of the few words of Welsh he knew as he replaced the receiver, and the obscenity was enough to push thoughts of the pompous assistant commissioner and his do-gooder wife out of his mind. And, as he hurriedly shaved and dressed, he allowed that he was prepared to drop his pressure for Drake Enterprises to be investigated by the Fraud Squad – for the time being. If anyone could provide the opener to rip the top off that particular can of rotten sardines, it would be Stark. And Stark would talk: Evans was in no doubt that he could make the kill-crazy little villain spill everything he knew – once the arm was put on him.

So it was that he had crossed the Channel in high hopes that Stark's days – maybe even hours – of freedom were numbered. For he had revised his earlier estimate of the fugitive's chances of staying on the loose in Europe. At that time it had been an emotive reaction to the disappointment of knowing the escaper had escaped again. Evans had simply seen an image of the map of Europe – a vast expanse of land mass with thousands of places to hide. But it wasn't so simple as that, of course. Stark was a Londoner who knew the city like the back of his hand: and an Englishman capable of merging into the background in virtually any part of the United Kingdom. His dossier contained the facts that he had taken French at grammar school and had driven on the Continent a few times when he worked at ferrying cars. He was, therefore, definitely not a jet-set cosmopolitan and as such would stick out like a sore thumb anywhere beyond his native country – the proverbial stranger in a strange land.

Such thoughts were the basis of Evans' enthusiasm as he was flown through the clouded sky towards Deauville. But the lack of progress by the French police dampened the superintendent's spirits. It was now almost dawn, many hours since the shootings at the cove, and Stark was obviously long gone from the town of Rouen where he had last been seen.

'Do we have anything on the girl?' he asked as the police car sped inland, south-east from the airport.

Manet was conscious of the mole on his chin, and he seemed to finger it constantly when he was not talking. He dropped his hand and his tired looking face took on a frown. 'The *agent* was sure she was French, superintendent,' he said. 'She spoke our language with a highly educated accent, but no foreign intonation. But the inspector and I have our doubts. The boat at the cove – the *Amanda* – belonged to a young English girl named Amanda Segal. There was a picture of her on board. Not a very clear one. The *agent* says he cannot be sure whether it is the same girl he spoke with. But he says it looks something like her. Interpol in London are trying to contact Miss Segal's family.'

'What about the dead men? Do we know who they are?' Evans was staring dispiritedly out at the Normandy landscape. It looked bleak and unfriendly in the dirty grey light of a dull daybreak. It struck him that death was an appropriate subject of conversation to match his mood of depression and the grim surroundings.

Manet's face, which gave the impression of being unable to wear a smile, confounded this idea. The humour it showed was slight, but the expression definitely conveyed amusement. 'A regular League of Nations, superintendent,' he replied. 'The man shot on board the boat was an Englishman named Peter Dunlop. So far we have been unable to trace any police record in France. He had a flat in Paris and apparently worked as a free-lance journalist, The man Louis Blanchard, whose death appears to have been accidental, was a Frenchman. He lived, as I said, in Rouen. He was something of a juvenile delinquent in the old days, but latterly he led an apparently blameless life as a garage proprietor. The man whose body was washed ashore in such a mutilated condition was Roger Putnam, an American. Black. His passport records he was a seaman and we assume that he was in charge of the boat.'

The police car swung to the east, but there was no early morning sunlight to dazzle the driver's eyes. Its destination was Rouen, where the detectives assigned to Interpol had set up temporary headquarters.

Shortly before they reached the end of their journey, a United States Consular official left the apartment of his mistress in a back street of Fontainebleau and hurried to where he had parked his car the previous night. He was up at such an early hour because his wife was returning from Berlin that morning and it was important that he be back at his Paris apartment for her arrival.

When he first saw the empty space where he had parked his car, he could not believe that the Mustang had been stolen. He walked, then ran, up and down the line of parked vehicles, certain the pleasures he had experienced in his girlfriend's bed had blunted his usually sharp memory. Only then, with a sinking feeling, did he admit the fact to himself.

The girl in the apartment above the shoe shop had enjoyed a virtually sleepless night and it took the American some time to rouse her with the door bell and his fist on the panel. She found the whole thing rather amusing, much to the chagrin of her nervous lover, who vented his anger on the unfortunate police sergeant who took his call.

The sergeant reacted by dealing with the complaint in a less than speedy manner and it was a full twenty minutes after the call was made before a weary-eyed *agent* pedalled into the street on his bicycle.

But the fatigue of night duty was abruptly pushed aside by the light of excitement as the policeman saw the Bedford five tonner parked at the end of the line of cars. The anxious American – prepared to shower the *agent* with verbal abuse for his dilatory attitude – found himself thrust aside as a second telephone call was made to the police station. This one resulted in much swifter action, producing a honking squad car carrying two plainclothes men of the *Police Judiciaire*.

His anxiety reaching frantic proportions, the owner of

the Mustang was restrained on the sidelines while the policemen examined the truck. Then he became the centre of attraction as he was questioned about the car, without being told the reason for the sudden increase in official interest. Finally he was asked – then ordered – to go to the local police station to make an official statement so that the red tape could be securely tied.

His mistress's amusement increased at the same rate as the American's rage, for he was the least satisfactory of her lovers in terms of the financial arrangements. It would be easy to replace him with an attaché from the Italian Embassy who was impatient enough to be very generous.

A length of red tape from the same reel as that which led to the American failing to be at home to greet his wife, also delayed the facts of the new development reaching the headquarters of the International Criminal Police Commission in the Boulevard Gouvion St. Cyr in Paris. But once the message was received by the bureau, no time was lost in relaying it to the trio of detectives at Rouen.

Superintendent Evan Evans, reluctantly drinking coffee out of a plastic container because the tea had proved so foul, was moderately cheered by the new information. The French police were still several hours behind Stark and the Segal girl, but at least they had not lost track of the couple completely.

CHAPTER FOURTEEN

The British detective was right not to be over-optimistic concerning the chance of recapturing Stark at an early date. The gap between the fugitive and his pursuers narrowed to three hours when the stolen Mustang was abandoned at Chalon in the Saône-et-Loire department. But there was a considerable delay in discovering that Stark and the girl had hitched a lift down the A6 autoroute to Lyons on an empty fruit truck. And an entire day was lost before it was established the couple left the city on a Cannes-bound express train.

Even when the trio of weary detectives completed their north-south crossing of France they could not be sure they had narrowed the search area down to a single town. The entire shoreline of the Côte d'Azur and the French Riviera – and the Italian frontier – was open to Stark and his girlfriend.

But Evans, at least, felt a little happier. The sky and the sea were almost a matching blue. The bright sun moved in a lazy arc on a long day's journey uninterrupted by cloud. The palm fronds on the boulevards moved only gently in the zephyr of a breeze. His eye wound was almost healed and the mild climate seemed to have a curative effect on his arm – it was still broken and immovable in the shell of plaster, but only painful when jolted.

Even the two French detectives experienced a lightening of their moods in the pre-season, relaxed atmosphere of the south coast. Because of their nationality, they were naturally more susceptible to intangibles than the unimaginative Welshman. And it was not so much that the change of climate and scene dulled the edge of their enthusiasm to catch up with Stark and the girl: rather that they shared a hunch the end was in sight. Like policemen the world over, neither Manet nor Bergeret was able to pin down a logical reason for feeling as he did about the case, but the conviction was there: Stark was close at hand and the time was getting ripe for him to show himself.

But both were experienced officers who knew that even the strongest hunch had to be backed up by routine police work. So police stations the entire length of the coast were circulated with an old prison photograph of Stark – augmented by the Rouen *agent's* description of the new-look fugitive – and a recent one of Amanda Segal supplied by her distraught father and wired to Paris by New Scotland Yard. The same material was given to the frontier posts at both the Italian and Spanish borders and airport and port security men in the area.

Then there was nothing to do but wait. This was not a practice which normally sat well on the broad shoulders of Superintendent Evan Evans, but he was forced to acknowledge that his French colleagues had done everything they could to cover all eventualities. And, although he never followed them himself, he was prepared to admit that a copper's hunch was not something to be dismissed lightly.

The Interpol men were not the only group waiting for Stark to reveal his whereabouts. West of Cannes, along the shimmering coastline of southern France, three men waited in a third floor room of a medium priced hotel behind the waterfront at Marseilles. They were René Léger, a prematurely bald thirty-year-old with an angelic face; André, his long-haired brother who was seven years younger; and Saïd Madani, an Algerian, fat and forty.

It was only a small room and they were all three big men – over five feet eleven and not one of them weighing short of sixteen stone. On the Algerian there was a lot of fat, but he was an expert marksman with the Luger Parabellum P.08 he carried in a shoulder holster. The Léger brothers specialised in the art of hurting people on a more personal basis. But if the circumstances did not allow them to get in close enough to use their strength, they could shoot fairly straight with the Mauser Hsc automatics – also carried in shoulder rigs.

When they registered at the hotel, the desk clerk had assumed them to be third-rate businessmen in town to close a deal. Which, in a way, they were: except for the rating. For their business was death and they were the top men in their field.

They were based in Paris where they were on the personal staff of Henri Calbiac, director of Drake et Cie., front organisation for the French section of the company. For most of the time, they were at Calbiac's château north of

Chartres or at his Rivoli apartment in the capital, working a shift system to ensure that the company's top man in France was constantly guarded. But the trio were always available for special duties when the necessity arose, and such an event was the killings and loss of a company cargo at the Normandy cove.

Although Stark had previously confined his vendetta against the company to Ralph Hooker's territory, his name was known to every branch of the organisation. And, just as Stark's activities in the United Kingdom had somewhat pleased Enrico Primo, so Henri Calbiac was amused that Hooker's reputation was being undermined. But when he learned that Stark had struck such a hard blow on French territory, Calbiac's pleasure was instantly changed to harsh anger. Despite Hooker's enviable record, which led to the man being so highly regarded at international level, Calbiac prided himself on running a pretty tight branch of the company in France.

The loss of the three men did not cause him so much concern. But the fact that three million francs' worth of cut heroin had been handed to the police on a plate was both a serious blot on his company copybook and an enormous financial loss personally. For the top man in each branch of the company was ultimately responsible for every operation within his jurisdiction. Thus, Calbiac would be required to make good in the international coffers the percentage of retail value which would have been expected from the sale of the heroin in the United Kingdom.

The anger this aroused in him was reflected in the speed with which he despatched the Léger brothers and Madani to assassinate Stark. The fact that the three gunmen arrived in Marseilles within an hour of the time the Interpol detectives reached Cannes was a mark of the French company's powerful fix with the police. They had no contact on the untouchable International Criminal Police Commission itself, but the bureau had to operate in close touch with the *Police Judiciaire* and the *Gendarmerie Nationale* in the gathering of information from the ground. And in both these branches of law enforcement there were more than enough officers with well greased hands to keep Calbiac in touch with the pursuit of Stark.

Once it had been established that the chase had led to the Mediterranean coast, Calbiac had instructed the gunman to make Marseilles their base. His reasoning behind this decision was simple, and based on the knowledge that the gun-running freighter *El Dorada* was heading for this port. It was the sole fact he had about the Vega-Primo gun deal, for Marette was the French company's representative at the negotiations and Calbiac had considered him capable enough to take care of things without need of reference to top level. It was not even a French sponsored project – France having been chosen for the negotiations simply because it provided convenient neutral ground.

Calbiac had no means of knowing Stark's actual intention in heading south. He had to assume that the renegade had somehow acquired knowledge of all current operations involving the French company. Having wrecked the narcotic smuggling venture, it seemed likely he would turn his attention to the *El Dorada* and her cargo.

So, like the trio on the other side of the law who bided their time in Cannes, the two French and one Algerian company men waited in Marseilles.

Their patience was rewarded at three-twenty on Wednesday afternoon when the *Police Judiciaire* headquarters at Nice picked up the details of the massacre in the pine forest north of town and telephoned the news to the Interpol men at Cannes. The instrument on the cabinet between the double and single bed in the third floor hotel room in Marseilles rang less than five minutes later.

Stark was out in the open – with a vengeance.

CHAPTER FIFTEEN

As Stark swung the Toyota around the final bend in the track between the aromatic pine trees and the tyres spurted dust from the surface of the café car park, the statuesque waitress stared at him in disbelief.

She was standing near the door at the top of the short stairway, minus her apron and clutching a lightweight topcoat in both hands. She was alone. There were no new cars parked to indicate patrons for the café and no sightseers attracted by smoke or shooting. An articulated truck and two cars sped past, heading down to the village at the head of the valley. Stark stomped on the brake and stopped the Toyota short of the road.

'*M'sieur*!' the girl shouted, starting down the steps. 'What has happened?'

A goggled and helmeted motorcycle cop flashed past, heading up the side of the valley. Behind him was a *Touring Club de France* breakdown truck towing the abandoned Renault, front wheels winched clear of the road. Fresh sweat broke out on Stark's forehead and along his upper lip among the bristles of his new moustache. He had been lucky. The sound of the exploding petrol tank and the shooting which followed had carried only as far as the café. The fire? He knew from having seen the puff of woodsmoke from the kitchen stove that evidence of the blaze was visible from a great distance. But how long before somebody decided it might not be a controlled fire tended by a ranger or the owner of the land?

'*M'sieur*? It is you!'

The waitress was running towards the Toyota, recognition spreading across her anxious face. Stark checked the road was clear and rocketed the car forward. The girl shouted something else, then pivoted and ran back up the steps. It was she who telephoned the police.

Stark gained quickly on the breakdown truck and its burden, straining up the steep incline. A length of straight road allowed him to overtake and it was with a feeling of relief that he saw the motorcycle cop had left his escort duty to speed on ahead.

The Toyota took the climb to the crest of the hill with ease, but the steering felt imprecise in Stark's skilled hands and he didn't trust the car on the tortuous twists and turns of the downward slope to the coast road. There was one bad moment, on the straight section of road that ran across the flat land on the final leg towards the tranquil blueness of the sea. Two police motorcyclists raced towards him from the opposite direction, headlights blazing at full beam through the heat haze. A squad car followed close behind. He sank lower in the seat as a reflex action, and realised the futility of such an action as the cops sped by. Then more headlights blazed, like reflections of the sun, and sirens blasted for passage priority. Traffic headed up into the hills swerved into the side of the road to allow three fire engines space to roar past.

The awesome sight of the police vehicles racing towards him had sent the blood pounding through Stark's veins and the sense of relief when they swept by, involving him only in the faint tug of slipstream which rocked the Toyota, could easily have left him in the grip of an exhilarating self-confidence. But he forced his mind to work coolly: to acknowledge that luck was a bonus of careful planning. Apart from being wanted by the French police, he had no doubt that the local company organisation was looking for him following the damage he had done up north. To drop his guard for a moment – unless he had every approach covered – could well prove dangerous, even fatal.

So he drove the car carefully, constantly watching the road ahead and behind for the first sign that any vehicle, official or otherwise, was showing an interest in the Toyota. And he made sure he obeyed strictly every road sign and traffic signal.

He crossed the A8 autoroute by an underpass and turned on to the coast road at Antibes. He cut across the neck of the Cap to Juan-les-Pins and began to worry about the rapidly emptying tank of the car. But the engine showed no inclination to die as the beach hotels of Golfe-Juan emerged out of the haze ahead of him. It continued to run sweetly up to the moment when he angled into the kerb beneath the shade of a palm tree and switched off the ignition.

The space he had chosen was immediately behind

another Renault R8, almost identical to the one he had abandoned on the valley road – differing only in that it was painted blue: and that Amanda had hired it from a local French company rather than Avis in Nice. The girl, seated behind the wheel, turned and waved cheerfully through the rear window at him.

Stark did not acknowledge the greeting. He looked down on the beach and saw a wide array of near nude bodies spread out to soak up the cut-price, early season sun. Then he glanced both ways along the boulevard. The strollers were not displaying quite so much flesh, but the mode was still casual. He slid out of the car, dragging the case of money after him. Two young girls in shorts and halters eyed him as if they could be interested in him and the car – providing he had a swinging friend.

He showed them a grin under his dark glasses. 'Forget it girls,' he said. 'I'm a fiend.'

The girls looked at each other in horror. 'He's bloody English,' the one with a love bite on her neck exclaimed. Apparently, they didn't care about the fiend part. They hurried away in search of Continental meat.

Stark went to the boot of the car and lifted the lid carefully, making sure the AR10 had not slid from under its cover of sacking. It was still hidden. He wrapped the gun and lifted it out. Then he closed the boot lid and sidled along to the Renault. Amanda saw he had both hands full and leaned across to push open the door.

'Behind the seats,' he instructed, thrusting the gun inside the car.

She took it and placed it on the floor in the rear. 'What is it, beautiful?'

'Remember our deal, darling,' he reminded her, dropping into the passenger seat at the front and resting the briefcase on his lap.

The girl made a face, but the expression was good-natured. Then she shot the car forward while Stark was still closing the door. She drove westward, picking up the A8 autoroute, swinging away from the coast and continuing in the same direction on the N7 from north of St-Raphaël. There were no instructions from Stark, for his part of the operation was completed. She, without knowing the details of what it was all about, had selected where they would go afterwards and had planned the route herself.

The 'no questions' deal had been made on the train journey from Lyon to Cannes. She had simply asked him, out of curiosity, why they were making a run for the south of France. Why not Switzerland? Or Italy? Portugal or Spain? He had replied, without rancour, that she could go and look for her kicks anywhere she wanted. No hard feelings. But if she wanted to stick with him, she had to learn to live without explanations.

Looking from the window of the speeding express, Amanda could see the peaks of the Maritime Alps jagged against the eastern skyline. They were capped by snow and suddenly she shivered, as if an icy draught had zoomed down from the mountains and struck only at her in the warm interior of the coach.

But her muscles were reacting to fear rather than cold, of course. She had encountered ruthless men in her short lifetime of swinging free with no thought for the consequences: but always their hardness had been tempered by a desire to secure exclusive rights to her receptive body. And it was because of this factor that she had always, up to this point, been in control. Even Peter Dunlop, who was the most dangerous – and therefore the most exciting – man she had ever possessed, could be reduced to a submissive animal if she chose to have him in such a way.

But now Stark had been promoted to the top of the league by the yardstick on which Amanda judged men: and she had quickly realised that over him she had no control. Born or made, he was a loner. He was a man, and therefore needed a woman to satisfy his natural urges. But any woman would do, provided she had the necessary equipment packaged to appeal to him. But even when she was forced to acknowledge this, Amanda was able to salve her injured ego with the belief that he needed her in another way – her knowledge of French and France was useful to him.

But the exchange on the train, as it rattled over the points at Grasse and began the final leg of the journey to the coast, exploded this conviction as a myth. Her superior knowledge was in the same class as her sexual prowess – there for the taking, but in no way indispensable. But it was not the mere fact that she was forced to admit defeat which filled her with dread: rather that in failing to have control over Stark, she had put herself under his power. For the consequences of this crazy experience with Stark were like nothing which had ever threatened her before. This was no kicking over the traces for a giggle or indulging her whims in an escapade with the insurance of daddy's money and influence to protect her against comebacks. She was on the run with a murderer, and by her actions was as guilty as he in the eyes of the law. Even daddy's money couldn't buy everything.

So she finished the train journey in a mood of depression and fear, knowing she had come too far to consider turning back: and aware that it was Stark who was in a position to indulge *his* whims. He could continue to use her, or he could leave her stranded. And that her fate was in the hands of a man such as Stark was a terrifying thought.

But the two days they spent at the five star hotel on La Croisette left her laughing at the miserable experience of the train journey. They registered as Mr. and Mrs. Michael Hodder and the hotel grapevine had quickly circulated the rumour that they were honeymooners. Thus, they were the objects of only the normal type of curiosity whenever they emerged from their suite. This was not often and they never explored further than the hotel's oval swimming pool to rinse away the perspiration of strenuous lovemaking and then soak up the rays of the sun to gain strength for the cycle to begin again.

Stark had seemed like a different man during those two days, showing not a trace of sullenness or ill-temper. And, by allowing him the dominant role in their couplings, Amanda discovered the ultimate pleasure. He became the teacher and she the pupil, with neither staking a claim as such. By Tuesday evening, she had forgotten why they had come to Cannes and had no inclination to consider what the future held. It was enough simply to be with Stark and his insistence that there should be no questions was not an irritation any more.

Amanda suddenly realised that, for the first time in her life, she might be in love.

So it was not like a bubble bursting when Stark called a halt to the idyllic interlude on Tuesday. She asked no questions when he went out of the hotel precincts for the first time and returned with a hired car. She was disappointed, but raised no objections when he refused to make love that night. Early rising was not a particular forte of Amanda's, but she made a big effort to appear cheerful when he roused her at six and they checked out of the hotel thirty minutes later, without the usual breakfast in bed.

The sun was already burning the mist off the sea when they reached Golfe-Juan but the air was still fresh with the cool after-taste of night. She felt cold almost as soon as he switched off the engine, killing the warm air from the vents. But she did not complain and listened carefully as he explained what she had to do. He asked the first question.

'We'll need a place to stay out of sight for awhile, darling. Away from the coast. Not a big town. Know anywhere?'

Amanda wished he would speak the word 'darling' with an intonation of genuine affection. He said it now in precisely the same way he had first used it when talking to her. Even when they were in bed together, he used the term of endearment in the same manner he would in talking to a waitress or hotel maid.

She had suggested a resort village in the Pyrenees where she had spent childhood holidays with her parents and he had agreed it sounded fine.

'How long will I have to wait for you?' She had posed the question in a tentative tone, but Stark had not taken exception to it. He had been pre-occupied and terse ever since he woke her at such an ungodly hour.

'Until I get here, darling,' he replied curtly, looking out of the window towards the long stretch of smooth beach, almost empty except for an elderly man tossing a stick for his dog. 'If you aren't here, it may or may not be important.'

Now he turned to look at her and a tiny pinprick of fear stabbed at her insides. His eyes were bluer than the Mediterranean, but looked much colder in the instant before he covered them with the Polaroids. She read a threat in the depths, but then dismissed it and the fear evaporated. She would wait, not because she was afraid of what he would do if she did not follow his instructions.

Rather because she was afraid of what she would do without him.

So she got out of the car and raised a hand in meek farewell as he made a U-turn and drove away towards Cap d'Antibes. The man with the dog came up off the beach and she went on to it, dragging her feet through the sand as she walked towards the tideline. The sun was beginning to make its warmth felt and soon the early season visitors would throng down from the hotels to deepen their tans. But for a few moments Amanda had the strip of beach and vast expanse of sea to herself and the void was a foil to her feeling of loneliness. Even when a speedboat rounded the Cap and cut a graceful arc of white water towards a jetty fingering out from the beach it offered no relief to the bitter-sweet mood which gripped her. The boat deposited a half dozen lithe, brown-bodied girls on the beach and shortly afterwards more girls paraded down from the hotels and spread themselves on richly coloured bath-towels and raffia mats. Next came the musclemen, ogling the curvatures of flesh from behind dark glasses.

Amanda watched it all and then left the beach with a sigh. Stark would coldly take any of the girls in exchange for her: but the bulging groins and rippling muscles of the handsome young men left her as cold as Stark's attitude. For now there could be nobody else except Stark.

So she was waiting outside the showroom of the car rental company when it opened and hurried the leering counter clerk through the formalities of hiring a Renault R8. She was parked on the tree-lined road alongside the beach at nine and left it for a short time only twice – once to buy *Time* and the *Riviera Sun* to help the minutes drag by and then to get an ice cream which served for lunch.

The veneer of cheerfulness with which she greeted Stark when he parked behind her was a hastily erected cover for the depression which went deeper into her with each hour that passed. But, once they were well on their way to the place she had selected, it was no longer a wafer-thin covering. For Stark's mood was light. Whatever he had done that morning, it had satisfied him and the coldness of his expression and attitude gradually melted away until he was almost the same as he had been during those two wonderful days at the hotel in Cannes.

He asked her to stop at a café in Aix-en-Provence. She

stayed in the car and watched him use the telephone in the cafe. When he returned to the car, he was exactly as he had been at Cannes.

'Let's go, Mrs. Hodder!' he yelled gleefully as he dropped into the seat beside her. 'It's a beautiful day and you look good enough to eat.'

'I'll always be on the menu for you, darling,' she replied, and shot him a sidelong glance.

His smile did not flicker. 'Who knows,' he said. 'Maybe the mountain air will whet my appetite for that kind of thing.'

Her inner thighs seemed to catch fire, feeding on the strength of her legs. Her foot slipped off the accelerator and a taxi driver behind had to stomp on his brake as the Renault abruptly lost speed. He honked angrily.

'Get stuffed!' Stark yelled.

Amanda regained control of herself and powered the Renault forward, rationalising that the faster they reached their destination, the sooner reality would replace imagination.

CHAPTER SIXTEEN

The Léger brothers and Madani did not move out of the hotel room in Marseilles when they heard the news of what had happened at the house in the pine wood. The moment René Léger replaced the telephone receiver, he lifted it again and asked for an outside line. He dialled a local number and repeated the description of Vega's Toyota. No other information was necessary. Plans had already been made.

The man he called ran a company-owned tour and travel agency with branches in every resort on the coast and inland, from Perpignan in the west to Menton in the east, and north to Avignon. This man made several telephone calls of his own and waited anxiously for a response as the trio of gunmen calmly shot dice on the floor of their room.

A coach driver based at Antibes spotted the parked Toyota at Golfe-Juan and a courier who worked at a beachside hotel was able to give a full report on the transfer of a man and some luggage from the Toyota to a Renault which had been waiting across the street for several hours. She had the colour and make of the car, but was unable to describe the driver beyond the fact that it was a red-haired girl. It was enough. The Renault was spotted by a guide showing a party of American schoolgirls over the Roman amphitheatre at Arles. The guide had a thing for under-age girls in ankle socks, but he tore himself away by feigning sickness and made a telephone call.

Before Stark and Amanda were halfway to Montpellier they were under surveillance from two cars whose drivers used the leap-frog technique as a guard against being spotted. Two more cars took over the surveillance as the Renault swung north through the failing light of evening towards the foothills of the Pyrenees. Stark had them tagged before the Renault was ten kilometres out of Montpellier.

He leaned over the seat and lifted the Armalite AR10, peeling off the sacking. The rust-resistant chromium plating gleamed in the headlights of passing cars and Amanda gasped.

'Christ!' she muttered.

'Eyes on the road, darling,' Stark warned. When she complied, he explained: 'I nicked it. From a man who may be dead by now. And even if he isn't, he won't be in a position to make any complaints.'

He snapped out the magazine and checked the weapon carefully, nimble fingers and agile brain working out how to fire the gun. When he was satisfied he had mastered the technique, he replaced the magazine and allowed the butt to rest on the floor between his feet, the steel barrel held by the press of his thighs.

'You should know we've got an escort,' he said after a lengthy silence.

Amanda began to breathe more heavily.

'Nothing to worry about,' he assured her. 'It's not the fuzz. They would have stopped us by now.'

'The company? You jumped the company again?' A threat from a third party allowed her to ignore possible repercussions from Stark.

'And how,' Stark replied, glancing idly out of the side window, across the grim profile of Amanda as a white Fiat swept by. It was one of the cars which was keeping track of the Renault.

He had explained all about the company on the journey south, before slamming closed the shutters on questions, but had given no indication of his intention to wipe out as much of the organisation as he could before it or the law stopped him.

'Christ!' she said again.

'They prefer to do things discreetly,' he said. 'Taking us out on an open road would be an emergency measure. Now they have us spotted, there's no rush. So just drive normally, as if nothing was wrong.'

Amanda gulped and shot a glance at him, then rapidly returned her frightened gaze to the road ahead. 'If you wanted that, why did you tell me about them?' she demanded softly.

Stark's lips cracked in a grin she couldn't see. 'I might be wrong, darling,' he told her. 'The French are supposed to be a pretty temperamental bunch. Could be one of the boys following us will get trigger happy and start blasting.

If something like that happens, you ought to know the reason.'

'Thanks,' Amanda said wryly. 'Thanks one hell of a lot.'

But nobody did get trigger happy. For the word was out that three of Calbiac's top men had been sent into the area with a special assignment to get Stark. So nobody was about to try to win any glory under those circumstances.

The Léger brothers and the Algerian checked out of their hotel room within seconds of the tour operator telephoning the information that Stark was still swimming free but was firmly in the net. A chauffeured limousine was waiting for them at the kerb and they were driven to a private airstrip north-east of the city. They boarded a Piper Navajo and the pilot was given clearance for take-off. He flew the aircraft up into a sky that was black with full night, sprinkled with diamond-bright stars and a moon that was waxing past the half. He levelled out at thirteen thousand feet and cruised at two-hundred-and-twenty miles-an-hour on a flight path towards the international airport at Toulouse. Behind him in the six-seater cabin the three gunmen field-stripped their pistols and slotted them back together.

When they had completed this chore, the pilot asked them if they would like a drink, but they declined politely. René said they had to go to work soon and they never drank when there was a job to do. Soon, the brothers drifted into sleep, lulled by the dull roar of the twin engines. The Algerian chain-smoked foul-smelling cigarettes.

As the navigation lights of the Navajo faded into the distant sky, the ungainly bulk of the freighter *El Dorada* appeared at the entrance of Marseilles harbour and was piloted towards a berth. The captain, a short, overweight Spaniard with a two-day growth of beard and the smell of rum on his breath, tried to conceal his nervousness. But he had sucked the bottle dry of liquid courage and it was still not enough to combat the knowledge of the cargo hidden beneath the crates of oranges in the holds. The smartly-dressed and ultra-efficient pilot saw the flaws in the captain's pretence but neither knew nor cared about the reason for the man's apprehension. He was concerned solely with ensuring that the *El Dorada* reached the dock-side safely.

On the quay, Manet, Bergeret and Evans watched from the shadows of a cold storage warehouse as the freighter slid, dead slow, into her mooring. They held their position while lines were tossed over the side and the warps were looped over bollards. Unlike the pilot, the dockyard workers did know of police interest in the ship and they completed their tasks quickly, first with the warps and then positioning the gangway. When this was done, they moved away quickly and Bergeret uttered a soft curse as two of the men broke into a run.

The pilot came down the gangway, the buttons of his uniform glinting in the yellow light from quayside standards. He reached the dock and his heels clicked sharply on the concrete.

'*C'est bien!*' Manet yelled.

Three searchlight beams stabbed harsh, accusing fingers at the ship. The pilot was rooted to the spot by shock. He was dazzled and held his hands up in front of his face. He heard shouting from the ship and from the quay. He peered between cracks in his fingers and saw the shapes of several uniformed men looming in front of him. He heard an instruction to get out of the way. When he did not comply immediately a strong hand gripped his upper arm and thrust him aside. He yelled and tripped, pitching headlong to the hard concrete, scraping his elbow and forehead.

A voice, amplified by electronics, was warning the *El Dorada*'s captain that police and customs men intended to board the ship. Any resistance would be sternly dealt with. The pilot shook his head, dazed by the rough treatment, and looked around him. The searchlights were mounted on trucks. Most of the shadowy figures he had seen emerged as CRS men in blue-black battle-dress, grim-faced and carrying revolvers. But there were a number of men in civilian garb. These moved forward in two groups, slightly behind the riot squad.

The pilot scrambled to his feet and began to scamper away towards the shadows behind the searchlights. The amplified voice continued to boom its demand for a boarding party to be allowed on the ship.

On the bridge of the *El Dorada*, the captain felt his

nervousness explode into panic. Vega's orders for such a situation as this had been specific. Surrender peacefully and keep a tight mouth. Arrangements would be made to get the captain and crew out of trouble.

But the captain did not trust Vega. He did not trust him further than he could see him and Vega had been a long way out of sight when, passing through the Straits of Gibraltar, the captain had ordered a case of rifles and one of ammunition to be opened. The rifles had been concealed, but close at hand, when the pilot was taken aboard. Now, as the police made their demands, every member of the ship's fifteen-man crew drew an AR10 from its hiding place and waited for the captain to make a move.

Even as he opened up with the first burst of rapid-fire, the drink-sodden brain of the fat captain realised the impossibility of winning anything by his action. But before a second burst of gunfire sounded from the forecastle, raking the quay and shattering all three searchlights, the captain saw the horrifying results of his wild shooting.

Two of the CRS men crumpled, spouting great gouts of scarlet blood from gaping holes in their faces. And two figures in one of the groups of plainclothesmen were thrown hard to the quay under the impact of high velocity bullets drilling into their chests. The captain was committed and he squeezed the trigger again, raking the barrel of the rifle back and forth in a wild frenzy.

Lying on the quay, his body numb, Superintendent Evan Evans listened to the shouting and the gunfire and his mind rushed back across the years to when he had been a detective sergeant during the blitz. But that was history and he shook his head to clear his brain. He found himself looking into the open, dead, staring eyes of Bergeret.

'Stark!' the British detective rasped, and felt a moisture in his throat which was stickier than spittle. 'You bastard, it's your fault.'

His eyes began to sting and he thought he was crying. But then he realised this was wrong as he distinguished the thudding reports of grenade launchers amongst the rattle of rifle and pistol fire. Tear gas canisters were being lobbed aboard the gun-running ship.

The honking of a French siren sounded far off, but drawing closer by the second. Manet stooped over Evans and tried to smile with a great deal of assurance. The mole on his chin looked enormous.

'An ambulance is on its way,' the French detective said.

Evans realised Manet was not shouting, then discovered the reason. The shooting had subsided and the siren had been turned off. There was a heavy silence hanging over the quayside and the freighter. It was broken by the policeman using the amplifier. There was a pause, then a stream of excited Spanish from the ship.

'We have asked them to surrender,' Manet explained to Evans. 'They say yes. The captain and at least three men are dead. Three more wounded.'

Evans felt a stab of pain in his chest. It was worse than anything he had experienced from his broken arm. 'How do I look?' he asked, unable to raise his head to examine the wounds himself. His mouth felt stickier than ever and his words had a liquid sound to his own ears.

Manet's eyes focussed upon the wide area of blood staining the front of Evans' shirt and jacket. Then he looked at the trickle of red cutting a course down the Welshman's chin, spilling from the corner of his mouth. 'Fine, *mon ami,*' he said, trying another smile.

But Evans saw the raggedness at the edge of the Frenchman's expression. And he felt the pain in his chest expand. He recognised the taste and texture of blood in his mouth. He knew a lung had been punctured. Stark had won. He heard footfalls and looked up. Excitement flooded him and he struggled to rise. Stark was standing over him. His head rolled and he saw Stark again. A different body, but it was Stark's face all right – looking sad as if he were sorry Evans had been shot. Then he looked at Manet, and it wasn't Manet any more. Stark, with a mole on his chin. Probably a disguise.

Evans opened his mouth to scream at the top of his voice for somebody to come and arrest Stark. But it was just a spray of blood that erupted from his lips. It fell back, warm, on to his face and ran into his eyes, blinding him.

'Mort,' Manet said sadly to the two stretcher bearers as he rose from crouching beside the dead British detective.

CHAPTER SEVENTEEN

Thursday dawned bright over the Midi-Pyrenees, warming the rugged rock faces of the mountains and soon chasing away the night chillness from the streets of the alpine villages. The sun probed illuminated fingers through the curtains at the window of a second floor room in the Hotel St. Michel overlooking one such village, to prise open Amanda's eyelids. She looked drowsily across the room and her sensual features took on the lines of a smile as she recognised the silhouette of Stark sitting in front of the window. Then the metallic glint of sunlight striking oiled steel brought her to full awareness and the smile disappeared in an instant, to be supplanted by fear.

'Anything, Stark?' she said in a hushed whisper.

'He's still up there,' Stark replied without turning to look at her. 'Stupid bastard's waving the binoculars around like a Boy Scout practising his signalling.'

The man he was talking about was perched among some pine trees on a slope above the other side of the village. As Amanda had driven the dusty and overworked Renault down the slope of the Aveyron hillside into the spa in the early hours of the morning, Stark had seen one of the two cars following them veer off on to a side road. The white Fiat had followed them all the way to the hotel.

Once in their room, Amanda had neither the opportunity nor the inclination to seek fulfilment of the half promise Stark had made earlier. Nervousness robbed her of the inclination and Stark ensured there was no opportunity by instituting a two-hourly shift system for keeping watch. He stood the first duty and spotted a splash of reflected moonlight across the valley, deciding it was caused by the window of a parked car.

Halfway through her two hours at the window, Amanda saw the flare of a match in the bushes close to the hotel pool. Now, as the sun chased darkness to the other side of the world, Stark was able to pinpoint the two watchers by the flash of sunlight on binoculars and the trail of grey cigarette smoke spiralling up from the clump of bushes beside the pool.

'What about the other one?' Amanda got out of bed and padded across to where Stark sat, taking care to avoid crossing in front of the window. She was naked, the white strips across her breasts and lower stomach emphasising the depth of tan she had acquired beside the hotel pool in Cannes.

Stark looked at her body hungrily and silently cursed the efficiency of the company in locating him so quickly. He had liquidated Ralph Hooker and achieved a bonus score against the company. It was enough for the time being and he felt he deserved a period of relaxation before planning his next attack. And there was nothing better than the luxurious Hotel St. Michel and the luxuriant flesh of Amanda Segal to ease the tension out of him. But with the company men staked out, watching the hotel, that could not be.

'He seems to be answering with Indian-type smoke signals,' Stark replied, putting an arm around her to rest his hand on the curve of her hip. But it was the only indulgence he allowed himself, tearing his gaze away from the thrusting cones of her breasts to concentrate on the sunlit scene beyond the window. 'They haven't moved all night.'

'Just watching?' she asked, dropping a hand to cover his, pressing it against her flesh. It was not a sexual move. More a gesture of her love for him and trust in his nearness to protect her.

'And waiting,' Stark said.

'For what, do you think?'

'Reinforcements,' he guessed. 'Or maybe for the experts to move in.'

Amanda took a peek out of the window and gave a rueful sigh. It would have been good here with Stark. Walking in the sloping, flower-carpeted meadows, exploring the caves, buying useless junk in the curio shops, taking the spa waters; eating, drinking, dancing and making love. She had fond memories of those holidays as a child, spent in this very hotel. Gentle nostalgia laced with new excitements had seemed a perfect mix in anticipation; and she was sure it would have proved so, had it not been for the sinister reflections and curling smoke on the edge of her ideal fragment of the world.

'Get dressed, darling,' Stark said suddenly, dropping his

hand from her hip and leaning forward to peer through the window.

She recognised a familiar tone of harshness in his voice and hurried to comply with the order, asking no questions. As she went into the bathroom, she heard the distant sound of an engine and then the crunch of gravel under turning wheels. From his vantage point, Stark was able to add visual images to the sounds and see the reactions to the new element in the peaceful vista.

A metallic grey Mercedes-Benz 280 SE had turned in off the road from the village and was gliding up the gravel driveway towards the hotel entrance. It carried a driver and two passengers, all men. No signals were exchanged that Stark was able to see, but the man among the ornamental shrubbery stepped into full view and strolled casually down to the road, like a guest commencing an early morning stroll. The Mercedes stopped and unfolded its doors. Far off, a starter motor whirred. There were more flashes of sunlight on glass against the greenery of the opposite hill. But moving now, as the second watcher drove away from his sentry post.

Stark stood up from the chair, pulled the curtains aside and pushed open the french doors. He stepped out on to the balcony and peered over the coping. The Léger brothers and the Algerian looked like tourists. They all wore white slacks and multi-coloured shirts worn jacket fashion. Madani even had a reflex camera slung around his thick neck. René supervised the unloading of three suitcases from the boot, handing them into the care of a porter. Then the men crunched across the gravel and into the hotel lobby. As Stark stepped back into the room, a car growled down the road towards the village. It was the white Fiat. He watched it go from sight around a bend, then emerge in the central square. It disappeared again, behind the church. He continued to watch, and saw it on the road snaking up the valley side to the hill crest.

Both watchers had withdrawn, their job completed. The executioners had arrived.

'Are we leaving, Stark?' Amanda asked, emerging from the bathroom.

She was dressed in flared pants and a loose fitting tunic which left her midriff bare. It was a white outfit, again accentuating her Riviera tan.

'After breakfast,' he replied, with a slight smile.

'They don't serve breakfast until eight,' she pointed out.

He brightened his smile. 'You don't seem to be wearing anything under that gear?'

She looked down at herself. 'I'm not,' she told him, surprised.

'So it won't take you long to get undressed again, darling,' he said. 'But I reckon we can think of something to fill in the rest of the time till eight.'

His eyes seemed to leave physical traces on her as they raked her from head to foot, his expression becoming more lustful with every plane and curve he drank in. And, despite her confusion at the abrupt change of plan, she felt herself react to his intimate scrutiny.

'You mean . . . ?'

'I mean we've got nothing to worry about for awhile, darling,' he supplied. 'The men sent to take us out walked in large as life, acting like henpecked husbands turned loose for a swinging sabbatical. So they aren't about to burst in on us and start shooting.'

As he spoke, Stark untied the cord on his dressing gown and shrugged his shoulders. The robe fell to the floor, leaving him naked and ready. Like the girl, his body showed evidence of almost complete exposure to the burnishing effects of the sun. Amanda gave a gasp of anticipation and hurriedly shed the tunic, then unzipped the pants at the waist and peeled them down her legs. The fine hair on her stomach caught the rays of the sunlight and sparkled like an illuminated pointer. She kicked the pants away and held open her arms. Her hands trembled, but the movement had nothing to do with fear.

As he approached her, she backed away, wetting her lips with a darting tongue. Her legs hit the side of the bed and she sat down. She fell back across the crumpled sheets, her breasts flattening to low mounds, her trembling thighs parting.

'Please, beautiful,' she begged, stretching her arms aloft, fingers crooked into claws.

Stark knelt down between the V of her legs and curled his arms around the underside of her thighs, his hands splaying across the gentle undulation of her stomach.

'Christ, Stark, yes!' she panted.

Her hands reached for him and she interlocked her

fingers behind his head, pulling him to her body. She still could not believe this was happening to her and in her anxiety her upper teeth pierced the skin of her lower lip. Stark had difficulty in believing it himself. As he experienced the perfume of her womanhood his mind was swamped with bitterness. Not aroused by Amanda; but arrowing from out of the past. For in all his countless infidelities, this was one act he had held sacred to Carol.

He screwed his eyes tight shut and his lips brushed flesh. Amanda moaned in ecstasy and acknowledged the reality by raising her legs and folding them about Stark. For a fraction of a second, the image of Carol was impressed on the dark retinas of Stark's blinded eyes. But as Amanda's body began to move against his face and her voice crooned softly in a mixture of groans and endearments, the ghost of Carol was relegated to its rightful dimension. A tender sanctum in his mind which would always be reserved for her memory. And suddenly the image was smiling, as if the ghost was happy that he had discovered living flesh to replace it.

Amanda released the grip of her legs and her hands dropped to his shoulders, gently tugging him up from the floor.

'I love you, beautiful,' she murmured as he complied with her wishes, encroaching the length of his body along hers. 'Beautiful, beautiful, Stark. Christ, why, why why . . . ?'

Her voice trailed away and then her breathing stopped as she fastened her lips to his. Her pent up breath exploded hot against his cheek as he entered her. Her legs interlocked around his back and the strength born of passion was exerted again as she arched her back, thrusting up to meet his driving force. Lust or love? Suddenly it mattered to her. Stark didn't know which.

At five past eight, André Léger looked up from a copy of *La Dépêche du Midi* and smiled engagingly.

'Bonjour,' he greeted.

'Hi,' Stark responded, showing his teeth in a smile, his eyes once more concealed behind the Polaroids.

Amanda nodded, unaware that the good-looking young man was one of the trio of executioners assigned to kill her. She preceded Stark in to breakfast, a little nervous, but her mood lightened by the suspicion that her love might be returned. Stark had not voiced it, but there had been something different about their love-making: an unselfishness on his part that just had to indicate a subtle development in their relationship.

'Are they in here?' she asked as they were seated by a window in the almost empty dining room.

'Let me worry about them, darling,' Stark told her.

While she used her French to order coffee and sweet rolls, Stark looked idly out through the glass doors of the dining room and saw André Léger using the house telephone at one end of the reception desk.

When breakfast was over, Stark led the way out into the lobby. None of the gunmen was in sight. But when they went outside and got into the Renault, Madani appeared at a corner of the building and angled across to where the Mercedes was parked. He still wore the slacks and casual shirt, but had put on a jacket. It was much warmer than when the trio had arrived. Only able to cast a quick glance at the Algerian, Stark could not spot the bulge of a gun.

'Anywhere in particular?' Amanda asked as she slid behind the wheel of the Renault, wincing as her bare back between the tunic and pants touched the hot upholstery of the seat.

'These Continental breakfasts are never enough for me,' he replied, adjusting the rearview mirror so he could see the reflection of the Mercedes on the far side of the parking area. The Algerian seemed to be torn between getting into the car and running back to the hotel. The problem showed on his fat features as a worried grimace. Then he sighed and smiled. Stark glanced out of the side window and saw the Léger brothers emerge from the shadowed lobby and cross the gravel forecourt, trying not to appear hurried. 'How about an early picnic lunch?'

Amanda giggled. 'Same appetiser?'

'Time and a place, darling,' Stark answered. 'It's not when and where I'm being shot at.'

'Christ!' Amanda exploded, and started to turn in the seat to look around.

'Just drive the car!' Stark ordered harshly, reaching across to turn on the ignition. 'Not fast. Nice and steady, just like you were off on a picnic. Stop somewhere in the village so we can buy the stuff.'

'But this is crazy,' she blurted out.

'You have to do it,' he pointed out, readjusting the mirror so that she could see what it reflected. 'The three characters in the Merc. If you run out on me now, I reckon they'll feel confident that two of them can take me. How long do you think you can keep ahead of the other one?'

She seemed about to hurl a retort at him, but the fight went out of her. 'I'm sorry, Stark,' she said softly. 'It has to be all the way, doesn't it? I had my chance to duck out.'

'So drive,' he urged gently.

She started the car rolling. The Mercedes held back for a few moments, then followed.

'One thing,' she said.

'Yeah?'

'When it's all over, will you tell me something?'

'What?'

'Why.'

'When it's all over, darling, I won't be around to tell you anything,' he said.

It was cryptic, but not insoluble. She gave a gasp to reveal that she knew what he meant. But when she looked at him she saw his features had hardened into the mask of cold detachment which she had learned to read as a sign that he had closed his mind to all factors which had no bearing on what he was thinking. She steered the car around a curve in the road and ran into the fringe of the village. The streets were narrow and cobbled. The doors and shutters of the houses were mostly closed and the first sign of life was in the square.

Three old men sat on a bench near the trickling fountain in the centre. Two middle-aged women tourists in walking boots and with rucksacks on their backs rose from the sidewalk table of a café and waited for the Renault to pass before crossing the roadway. The solemn-faced owner of a pâtisserie stood outside his shop. Next door, a wine supermart was just being opened by a grinning boy.

Stark instructed the girl to angle the car to the kerb outside the shops, then told her to buy the basic essentials of a picnic. The Mercedes swept by and turned from sight around the church. The younger Léger brother waved cheerily at Amanda as she crossed the pavement to enter the baker's shop. She had the presence of mind to smile back. Stark got out of the car and went to the boot. He unlocked it and lifted out the sacking-wrapped rifle. He left the briefcase where it was.

He had hidden his loot in the car after parking it in front of the hotel the previous night. The decision had been made in the light of the possibility that a fast getaway might prove necessary. Also, it looked better to arrive at the hotel with no luggage at all rather than a briefcase and the odd-shaped bundle wrapped in sacking. Payment in advance and a flip lie about their cases being lost at either Heathrow or Nice airports had satisfied the hotel receptionist. He had even been sympathetic enough to find some nightclothes for the couple.

Stark was back in his seat, with the gun on the floor in the rear, when Amanda returned, laden with a large paper bag and two bottles of wine. The bag emanated a delicious odour of fresh bread and strong cheese as the car started rolling again.

The road which led off the square at the side of the church was the only one out of the village which did not dead end at an hotel or peter out into a narrow walking path into the hills. It climbed steeply up the wooded side of the valley to a T-junction, offering a route to the north-west or south-east. The Mercedes was parked on the verge close to the junction. René and André Léger were perched on the bonnet while Madani took photographs of them, with the village spread picturesquely in the background.

'Say hello,' Stark urged.

Amanda pressed the horn button.

'Turn left,' Stark instructed, waving at the trio, who hurriedly broke up the photographic session and piled into the Mercedes.

'Isn't there a chance we'll overdo the bonhomie bit?' Amanda asked nervously as she turned the corner and the engine began to struggle against the cant of the upgrade.

'There won't be time,' Stark answered absently, looking ahead and to left and right.

On one side the ground fell sharply away towards the village which already seemed to be made up of tiny model houses and hotels. On the other was a more gentle, rising slope of verdant meadows featured with stands of trees. It was in such a clump that one of the guards had stood his sentry duty through the night. Ahead, the road continued to climb, the steepness forcing Amanda to drop down to second gear. Then it flattened out and swung away from the valley, across an upland plain. It ran straight for three kilometers, then began to twist and turn, rise and fall. At first the terrain was open moorland giving sustenance to a few rugged looking sheep and goats. Then they passed a dairy farm and a few isolated villas. The Mercedes was a constant fixture initially, but when the road began to meander through a thickly wooded national park it was often out of sight.

Many hard-packed dirt roads led off into the park on either side and Stark warned the girl he would order a turn when the time was right.

'Now, left!' he shouted after several seconds turned in his seat, looking out at the road behind the car. 'Foot down hard.'

Amanda went into the turn in top gear, then fumbled down into second. The Renault shot forward, engine shrieking in protest. Stark cursed, continuing to concentrate on what was behind the car. The Mercedes had still been hidden by a bend in the road when the Renault changed direction. And when the track swung to the side, it took the Renault out of sight before the Mercedes glided by.

'Women drivers,' Stark said, a hint of humour in his tone.

'I'm not used to shaking gangsters off my trail,' Amanda defended, pleased that she had done everything he asked, more or less perfectly.

'Let's not make it too difficult for them to find us again,' he said. 'Park over there.'

He pointed to a small glade, carpeted by dark green grass dappled with sunlight through the branches of surrounding trees. A brook made cool rippling noises on the far side as the Renault stopped and the engine was switched off.

Stark lifted the gun from the rear and unwound the sacking as he climbed out of the car. 'Okay,' he said with a grin, flicking the catch to rapid fire. 'Over by the stream will be a good place. Spread out the goodies, then take your pants off.'

Amanda gulped. 'Christ, Stark,' she muttered.

André was driving the Mercedes and reacted quickly to his brother's demand for greater speed. In the rear seat, the

Algerian leaned forward anxiously. All three were concerned that the Renault had been out of sight for a long time.

The big V-eight engine responded well to the pressure of André's foot on the pedal and the car surged forward with only a slight rise in engine noise. The flat radials hugged the road in a tight rubber grip as the big car was drifted into bends and roared out of them. One such bend fed out into a straight stretch of tarmac which tapered into the distance for perhaps three kilometers. The woods on each side were fenced off. Notices proclaiming *Réservé* were fixed to the fences at regular intervals.

'Merde!' the Algerian exclaimed.

'Bâtard!' André hissed.

'Nous retournons,' René instructed.

André nodded and stomped on the brake. The tyres screeched, then gave a series of short shrieks as André jerked at the automatic shift and wrestled with the wheel, foot swinging from one pedal to the other, manoeuvring the big car around in a ten-point turn on the narrow road.

René told his brother to drive slowly, and instructed the Algerian to watch the side tracks on the right. He examined those on the left. It was Madani who saw the place where the Renault had turned off. The pointer was a swathe of dust spewed across the road from the track as the car's nearside rear wheel had inscribed an arc. The pattern of the Mercedes' tyre tread was printed in the dust.

The big car turned on to the track from the opposite direction and André braked when instructed to do so, pulling in close to one side. As René climbed out, he jerked the Mauser from his shoulder holster. André emerged with his right hand wrapped around the butt of an identical automatic. The Algerian's meaty fist somehow made the Luger Parabellum look smaller than it was.

René held back for a moment, and restrained his brother. Madani was the crack shot and it was therefore his task to take the initiative from here on in. The overweight Algerian accepted the prerogative and its inbuilt dangers with no outward show of anxiety. And, in truth, at times like these he had no nerves. He had fought as a mercenary in too many wars; killed too many men in the commission of countless crimes on four continents. So when danger surrounded him, it was almost a friend, holding no terrors. One killed or was killed. It was kismet.

But one did not invite death by foolish action: and taking the attitude of the enemy for granted constituted foolhardiness. So Madani did not assume that he and the Léger brothers had the element of surprise on their side.

He moved forward slowly, cautiously; using every piece of cover which presented itself. And he glowered a rebuke at each accidental sound made by René and André. When the parked Renault came into view, he crouched behind a bush and eyed it suspiciously for long seconds, watching for the slightest movement to betray occupants. Satisfied, he crept forward, hearing a sharp intake of breath from behind him as the brothers spotted the car. When the glade came into sight, Madani angled away from the track, into the trees with their soft carpet of rotted leaves from past autumns. Despite his bulk, the Algerian moved with the silence and litheness of a hunting animal of prey.

The sound of the rushing brook reached his ears and he halted again, going into a crouch when he saw the hunks of bread, cheese and pastries spread on the torn bag at the bank. He saw something else – white – nearby, but could not make out what it was. He looked over his shoulder and gestured with his hand for the brothers to stay where they were. René nodded in acknowledgement. André ran his coat sleeve across his sweat-beaded forehead.

The Algerian went forward on all fours, looking more than ever like a stalking animal. He reached the bank of the stream. It was clear and shallow, magnifying the size of the tiny fish darting among the water-rounded stones. He saw two bottles of wine sticking up above the surface close to where the food was set out. He felt suddenly thirsty, but the sparkling water had no appeal.

His eyes, black as coal, crinkled almost closed against the dappled sunlight, raked the clearing. They took in the trail of bent and broken grass blades from the car to the brook bank; then another, angling to the far side of the glade. He stood up and stepped out of his cover, the Luger extended in front of him, wavering from side to side in controlled sweeps of the ground and trees ahead. He reached the place where the food was set out and stooped, bending at the knees and waist. His free hand picked up the white object which he had failed to recognise from the fringe of the clearing. He glanced down at it, then at the ground. He cracked his mouth in a lecherous grin. He was holding the white pants and he let them fall, to again cover the sandals on the grass.

The grin broadened as he turned towards where the brothers were concealed, straightening his body. Then he made an unequivocal motion of his hips and stomach, backwards and forwards.

'*Jig-jigging, eh!*' he called softly.

He beckoned with the Luger and the brothers emerged from among the trees, side by side, Mausers at the ready. André responded to the Algerian's humour with a grin of his own. René's face wore a grim expression. He had the senior ranking in the company and the success or failure of the assignment was ultimately his responsibility.

'Saïd –' he began his instructions.

It was the last utterance he made. Death rained down from the tree tops in the form of high velocity bullets streaming from the muzzle of the AR10. Three shots punched a gaping hole in the top of René's skull, killing him instantly. He fell like a log, blood and brain matter frothing from the top of his head.

André screamed in terror and spun around, looking upwards. But he was dazzled by sunlight. A second burst of automatic fire exploded and three holes were opened in the younger Léger's stomach. He doubled over and fell backwards, splashing into the stream. He thrashed about in agony, draining away his lifeblood to turn the rushing water pale pink.

The Algerian squeezed off one shot from the Luger before the Armalite was turned on him. He took four bullets, two ripping open his thick throat, another thudding into his shoulder to pivot his falling body and the third spurting blood from his groin. He sprawled across the food, his blood turning the bread a moist scarlet.

For several seconds, Stark retained his position, perched high in a gnarled oak tree, the lightweight automatic rifle butt nestled against his shoulder, back braced against the trunk and feet wedged on two splayed boughs. By then, it was obvious that none of the assassins was going to get up. André continued to twitch in the shallow water, but by the time Stark had dropped to the ground, even he was still, the brook rippling around his body as if it was just another piece of rock to be worn smooth.

Stark fingered one side of the unfamiliar moustache as he crossed to the bank of the stream. His expression as he looked down at the blood-soaked bodies was one of mild satisfaction. But he did not gloat over his kills. He had involved himself in a war, with everything that entailed in terms of getting the enemy before the enemy got you. He had won this battle, but that was all it was. A battle. The enemy was much more powerful than three men and it had all the resources necessary to plan retaliation. And the plans would be made. Stark had to ensure they were not executed.

He heard a slight sound behind him and he turned slowly, knowing he would see Amanda. She was walking cautiously across the glade, inching her bare feet forward. Her nakedness extended from her feet to the hem of the tunic which reached only halfway down her flat stomach. She approached so slowly because she could not see where she was going. Her face was covered by her hands and he guessed she had her eyes tightly closed.

'I can't look, Stark,' she said with a tremor in her voice. 'At the cove was enough.'

Stark picked up the pants. 'Put these on,' he said, tossing them towards her. 'If the fuzz turn up we could get arrested for lewdness – or something.'

The pants curled around her upraised arms and neck. She turned her back on the scene of carnage before struggling into the pants. A bird tested a tentative chirp against the silence which had blanketed the wood since the shooting finished. Another bird answered with a whistle. The stream drew the final drop of blood it could get from André's twisted body and ran clear.

Stark picked up Madani's Luger and René's Mauser. André had taken his gun into the shallowness of his watery grave. He also recovered Amanda's sandals and carried his burdens to the Renault. The girl waited there, eyes open and uncovered. But she did not look towards the bank of the stream where the inevitable flies were zooming in for an early and unexpected lunch.

She made to open the door, but Stark shook his head. 'You'll drive?'

'Yeah, but in style, darling.'

He gave her the sandals and when he had opened the boot, made her carry the briefcase. He toted the minor arsenal of weapons. She trembled a great deal as the first few kilometers were eaten up by the Mercedes' eager wheels. But she managed to hold back the sobs.

CHAPTER EIGHTEEN

Henri Calbiac's château was thirty kilometers north of the Beauce region's market town of Chartres, south-west of Paris. It had been the country house of a mid-nineteenth century industrialist who had spared no expense on the house itself, the landscaped gardens and the artificial lake which lapped at the foot of a stairway from the french windows of the drawing room.

In exterior design, the château was a mock-Gothic monstrosity of discordant angles and curves. But the interior refurbished and redecorated under the stringent direction of Calbiac himself, was the ultimate in spacious luxury living for the latter half of the twentieth century. It had thirty rooms, twenty-eight of which Calbiac used for living and playing. From the other two, he ran that part of the business of Drake et Cie. which produced four times the profit of the front company. But only a restricted group of men knew about these figures for they never appeared in the books or published accounts of Drake.

However, Calbiac reflected as he sat in a swing lounger on a balcony of the east wing of the château, the company's tax-free wealth could not be tapped to make good the loss caused by the murdering Englishman named Stark. The stealing of two hundred thousand dollars of Italian company money had been bad enough. But then the *bâtard* had tipped off the *gendarmes* about the shipment of guns and they had been impounded. So Calbiac had been required to write a double sized cheque against his personal fortune, in order that the Italians could be recompensed and a fresh supply of contraband arms purchased for the waiting Arab guerrillas.

'You are not yourself this evening, *mon chéri*,' the girl said sadly.

She was English, seventeen-years-old and would be a beautiful woman in the distant future. Now she was merely extremely pretty, with saucer blue eyes, dimpled cheeks and pouting lips, the delicately formed features framed by jet black hair that reached to a mid point at her back. Her figure was still developing, but had reached the stage at which Calbiac found women most attractive – gently curved breasts which needed no support, a narrow waist flaring only slightly to hips and rump, and long, slim legs. Her flesh was firm and her skin very white: and Calbiac admired this, too, finding it much more attractive than the burnished, almost hard-textured bodies of the sun-worshipping women he had pursued as a young man.

'A problem, my sweet,' he replied in heavily accented English. 'Come, help to relax me into forgetting about it.'

The girl, whose name was Jennifer Darwin, smiled to conceal her revulsion and stepped away from the balcony rail. She was naked except for the bottom half of a bikini which was merely a token strip of shaped rubber held by a ring on each hip.

Calbiac wore nylon shorts but these slid from him easily as he lifted his rump from the lounger and the girl knelt before him and hooked her slim fingers over the waistband. Naked, there was only one physical part of the man which was not hard. He was five feet six inches tall and stockily built, with bulging muscles at his shoulders, chest, on his upper arms and legs. His body had been developed when young, working as a coalminer in the pits south of Lille. He had then learned of less arduous ways to earn more money in the protection racket. His elevation through the ranks of the company to the top position in France had been slow but sure. And he had never allowed the excesses available to him to mar his physical fitness, counteracting over-indulgence with a daily routine of exercise. Even now, at the age of fifty-five, he spent an hour every day either rowing on the lake or working-out in the gymnasium, converted from what used to be the château's ballroom.

The hard, muscular flesh of the powerful body was almost entirely matted with a covering of black hair, from throat to ankles and the backs of his hands. And he retained a fine head of hair which he kept neatly trimmed and greased with a parting on the right. The flesh of his face was also hard, heavily wrinkled but with no sacs of loose skin. It had never been a handsome face, for the basic structure was all wrong – overhanging brow, prominent cheekbones and square jaw. And the eyes were too small and too deep set, the mouth too wide and the nose undersized.

But the big and easy money which had come to him following his change of trade was increasing compensation for nature's unkindness. So he could afford to ignore those women who recoiled from his ugliness, for his wealth and connections ensured an unlimited supply of nubile young girls like Jennifer Darwin. Of course, he thought as he looked down at the top of her head and experienced a slight stirring in response to her busy mouth, she and most of the others like her probably detested him. But this served only to heighten his pleasure from them. For it was a mark of his power that he had only to make a demand and it would be satisfied: that was one of the greatest joys of his life.

Except that the rule had not proved infallible – Stark was still alive and free!

'You're no bloody good!' he exploded suddenly, putting both hands on top of the girl's head and shoving her violently away from him.

Jennifer was flung up on to her haunches and then thudded on to her back across the mosaic tiles of the balcony. Her pouting lips, still formed into the perfect circle necessary to comply with the hirsute man's former wish, emitted a thin cry of shock and pain. She looked up into his angry face with the pathetic expression of a dumb animal unable to comprehend an undeserved rebuke from its master.

'Get some bloody clothes on and fetch mine!' he demanded, leaping to his feet. 'The blue sharkskin suit, white shirt, black knit tie and black patent shoes. You wear the white dress with the high neckline.'

He glowered out over the lake, rippled by a slight breeze and sparkling with the dying rays of the sun slanting in over the roof of the house.

'We're going out, Henri?' Jennifer asked nervously, her big eyes staring up at him, seeing the rapid clenching and unfolding of his fists and the tremble of his lower lip which betrayed the fact that his violent rejection of her was not the climax of his rage.

'We're not going to play Scrabble, you stupid bitch!' he yelled down at her. 'Move your bloody self.'

Calbiac splayed both hands on the balcony parapet and fought to control himself. It was difficult, for he could not rid his mind of corrosive thoughts about Stark. Even though ten days had gone by since the Léger brothers and the Algerian had failed in their task of taking him out and the massive cheque had been written and cashed, his hatred for the Englishman had not abated a fraction of a degree. In fact, it had become more sharp.

Asking that Jennifer Darwin be brought to the château had been a last resort in attempting to salve his all-consuming enmity. In retrospect, he could see the futility of such an action. The fact that she was British – just as Stark was – meant nothing in the context of Calbiac's desperate need to exorcize the hatred he felt for the renegade. But Stark was untouched by it all. Once, he had come within a split-second of killing her before reason prevailed.

'Here are your clothes, Henri,' she whispered.

He turned and saw she had donned the dress he had specified. It made her look virginal, almost childlike. She carried his clothes over one arm and held the shoes in her hand. Fear showed deep in her big eyes and her smile was wafer thin, on the point of bursting wide open to reveal the terror behind it.

'You will dress me,' Calbiac said in an ice cold tone which she recognised as a further sign that his anger had still to be undammed.

'Yes, Henri,' she answered submissively, approaching him.

'We will then go to Paris,' he told her when she had draped the clothes on the lounger and knelt down in front of him to pull the underpants up his hair-matted legs. 'To The Menagerie Club, I think. Maurice tells me that Jacques is no longer showing so much interest in the black girl. He thinks it is because the girl has been made too big.'

Jennifer's whole body began to tremble and Calbiac roared with obscene laughter. And it was this that provided the release valve for his rage. But it did not offer any relief for the girl. She would much rather he had beaten her or ordered her down into the gymnasium to take part in another humiliating exhibition. Anything except The Menagerie Club and Jacques. For Jacques was a . . . a . . .

She was thrusting Calbiac's outstretched arm into a shirt sleeve when the enormity of her horror exploded into an action. She gave a thin wail and lunged away from him, springing towards the balcony parapet with her hands clawed. She got her fingers hooked over the coping, preparing to launch herself up and over. The warm air offered a welcome and the dark waters of the lake in the shadow of the house made soft gurgling sounds which seemed to croon encouragement. Death opened its arms to despair. But she was cheated.

Calbiac, moving with the speed and strength gained from his work-outs, pivoted and lashed at her with his free hand. He chopped her sharply across the base of her neck and Jennifer's flowing hair had little cushioning effect against the blow. The lights of consciousness went out and she didn't feel the pain of her fractured jaw as her chin thudded against the coping. She crumpled to the tiled flooring and remained still.

'Stupid bitch!' Calbiac hissed, and spat into her pale, composed face.

Stark hated Paris. He had been in the French capital on three previous occasions and been told that even the most disenchanted and blasé could not fail to fall in love with the city in springtime. But he had been in Paris for seven days now after driving leisurely across country from the south-west corner of France. The sun had shone for ten hours each day, the trees along the boulevards were in variegated blossom and the women were at their most *chic* in the new season's clothes. But, as during those former visits, he found the legendary atmosphere of the city cloyingly phoney. Notre Dame, the Louvre, the Arc de Triomphe and the Eiffel Tower seemed more than ever like fairground sideshows specially erected to hook the tourist punters. He could not shake free of the impression that the Gauloise smoke was pumped into the air by the city corporation because Paris was expected to smell of it; that the traffic cops and taxi drivers were putting on an act of over-excitement, and that the Latin Quarter was made of papier-maché.

That he was in no mood to enjoy anything was a factor in his present dislike, he admitted to himself as he smoked a cigarette and sipped a Scotch and soda in his third floor room in the Hotel George V. It was a single room and Amanda had never entered it.

It had not taken the girl very long to recover from the violence in the Aveyron national park. First there had been the excitement of high speed in the stolen Mercedes, then the nights of adventurous love-making at hotels in Limoges and Tours, and finally the extravagances of buying a new wardrobe in Paris. This had blotted out memories of the past. Stark's attentiveness and tender consideration for her feelings and wishes had wrapped her in a cloak of security for the present. And she forced herself not to think of the future until he raised the subject.

He did so as they sat at a pavement table outside a café on the Champs Élysées after the shopping expedition.

'I need to get the big man, darling,' he said suddenly, his voice low but resolute.

The café was crowded, inside and out. A lot of the patrons were obviously British and American tourists. Amanda kept her own tone soft.

'Isn't the killing ever going to stop, Stark?'

He sighed. 'I told you about that, didn't I?'

She could recall his exact words: *When it's all over, darling, I won't be around to tell you anything.*

Her sensual features took on a pained expression. 'Why? What is it, Stark? Some kind of death wish?'

'They made it,' he answered. 'Although they didn't know that's what it was.'

'Christ, Stark, it's stupid,' Amanda accused with a trace of low-voiced anger. 'Who do you think you are – some kind of avenging angel protecting society from evil? We pay police forces to do that for us.'

Stark sensed his own anger rising and he didn't reply for several moments. He stared out through the strolling pedestrians to the crawling traffic, struggling to check the threatened explosion of his emotions. Then he looked back at Amanda and it was her expression of mixed pleading and confusion that calmed him. He felt something for this girl: not strong enough to be termed love. But his attitude towards her over the past three days had not been entirely based on an ulterior motive.

'Okay,' he said softly. 'If you want me to justify myself, okay. It's nothing to do with that guardian of society crap, though. If people want to get stoned out of their minds on horse, LSD or any other kind of junk, that's their business. If the Arabs and the Jews want to blast each other to hell, ditto. If guys want to get rooked by bent roulette wheels or pay over the odds for their oats so the pimps can get a slice off the top, that's all right with me.'

He paused to light a cigarette. It was a British brand and the aroma had no chance against the blue and grey smoke drifting across the tables. 'The crooks and hoodlums stay in business because that's the way the punters want it. But I'm not a punter. And I never was. I was on the receiving end of the easy money. But the bastards double-crossed me. Worse. They killed somebody I loved. And were directly responsible for taking out my parents, who I may have loved. So I'm an avenger or a revenger or something like that. But for me – nobody else. The way it's set up, I'm on a trip to nowhere. Once I killed the first company man and cracked open a company operation, I went to the head of their take-out list. So even if I wanted to call a halt, I couldn't. Because the company will never let up on me. But it so happens I don't want to call a halt. I want to take out as many of them as I can before they get me.'

Amanda felt unreal. The traffic in the street, the café and the people at the tables were all solid actualities. But she – and Stark – were ectoplasmic beings in somebody else's bad dream. It was just not possible that in real life a handsome young man could sit across a table from her in a public place, smiling a fixed smile and calmly smoking a cigarette as he explained his determination to kill countless perfect strangers before one of them killed him.

But then the memory of the bloodied bodies by the stream flooded her mind and she admitted the truth of her situation.

After that, it had been easy for Stark. They left the café and took a taxi to Porte Dauphine. He told her what he wanted her to do and she agreed without complaint. He said she didn't have to – that he would give her ten thousand dollars and they could go their separate ways. But, as they sat on a bench beside Lac Inférieur in the Bois de Boulogne, she knew that she had committed herself to staying with Stark: had come too far to try to back out now. It was all or nothing, and without Stark there would be nothing: despite what he was.

So, while he registered at the Hotel George V, she moved into a cheap *pension* on a back street in the night club area. He spent his days eating, drinking and watching television – between catching up with the news. He learned with satisfaction of the raid on the gun-running ship. He felt no more regret for Evans' death than that of Vega, the latter shot down in a hospital ward. The abandoned Mercedes was found on the outskirts of Paris and the empty AR10 on the back seat provided a link with the bloody glade and the *El Dorada*. But the police had to admit they were baffled. Stark slept peacefully at nights.

By contrast, Amanda rested during the days and at nights made herself attractively available in smoke-filled bars and cellar clubs. The environment appalled her, but the acting came easily. She had had a lifetime's rehearsal.

She telephoned Stark on the morning of the third day to report that she had been approached by a man with a more interesting offer than money for her time. He ran a café with a large upstairs room used for stag shows. Stark told her to follow through. If the operation was big enough, it sounded like something in which the company would have an interest. She called back the next morning: it was a big operation. A regular three shows a night for an audience of at least fifty, each paying one hundred francs for admission. The entertainment commenced with a blue movie and finished with bi-sexual acts in the flesh. Amanda had been offered a part as a stripper: no participation in anything else unless she wanted the extra money.

Again Stark gave her the go-ahead, this time with a sense of anticipation that his objective was getting closer. But as the time slipped slowly by, his distaste for Paris grew into bitterness. He refused to acknowledge that it was his own fault – not that of the city – Amanda was taking off her clothes three times a night before the leering eyes of frustrated punters.

When the telephone shrilled and he rose to answer it, he staggered and felt a stab of anger at himself when he saw the level of whisky in the bottle. Never before in his life had he found it necessary to drown his regrets in drink. It was another mark he could chalk up against the company.

'Hodder,' he said into the mouthpiece, saying the alias very distinctly, making a conscious effort not to slur.

'It's me,' Amanda whispered in his ear, her excitement audible in the hushed tone. 'I'm going up in the world.'

Stark shook his head to try to clear the fuzziness in his vision. 'How?'

'A freaky queer named Maurice Murville was in the

audience of the final show last night,' the girl answered, her tone still low. 'Seems he thinks I'm better than the joint I'm in. And what he thinks is more important than what my boss says. I've got an appointment to see Murville at The Menagerie Club at eleven tonight.'

'Can you handle it?' Stark asked tightly.

For the first time, a hint of nervousness crept into Amanda's voice as she answered. 'The acts in my place get pretty rough for the girls who get paid the most,' she said. 'And I'm told they get peanuts compared with the girls at Murville's club. I'd like an escape route – just in case.'

Stark immediately felt sober. 'Give me the address,' he snapped.

She gave it to him – a side street off St. Germain Boulevard in the Latin Quarter.

'Don't look out for me,' he instructed. 'I'll see you.'

'Stark?'

'Yeah?'

'I miss you.' It was a plea.

'I'll see you,' he replied. It was a promise.

He rattled the receiver back on the cradle and crossed to the heavily ornamented wardrobe. The briefcase was under the two suitcases containing the clothes he had bought for Amanda. He left the suitcases and went out of the room carrying the briefcase. Inside was the two hundred thousand American dollars, most of what remained of the money he had brought from England, and the two automatics taken from the dead assassins.

Stark did not know whether he would be returning to the hotel, and the briefcase contained everything that was important to him. Except a sexy redhead named Amanda Segal.

CHAPTER NINETEEN

It was a warm night and the sky was clear over the city. But all except the brightest stars were invisible through the glow of street lights and neon which fought a losing battle against the dark.

Amanda, dressed in a black leather mini-skirt and high-necked, tight-fitting white sweater, paid off the taxi driver and took a deep breath before crossing the pavement to the doorway. She experienced a desperate desire to look around her, perhaps to catch a fleeting glimpse of Stark; but she resisted it. Although she felt sure there could be no danger in such an action, it would be against Stark's instructions. And she had to do exactly as he said, for he owned her – body and soul. Why else would she have undergone the experiences of the past three nights? Sex was supposed to be fun and, since sharing intimacies with Stark, she had discovered it could be beautiful. But the uses to which it was put at the club made it evil and dirty. And she felt tainted by her minor role of arousing vicarious thrills as part of the build-up to the obscene finale.

'Maurice is expecting you, *mademoiselle*.'

The unmarked door had a glass spy-hole in the panel and Amanda realised her arrival had been watched. For the door had opened without her having to knock and a girl with an unattractive face and the largest breasts Amanda had ever seen was smiling out at her. She wore black fishnet tights and a tunic laced at the waist and designed to thrust her mammaries high and forward, emphasising their enormity.

'I must have been described well,' Amanda replied, stepping inside as the girl beckoned her to do.

She laughed. 'I was told a girl was coming,' she explained. 'For an audition. All the girls who work here already use the rear entrance.' She laughed again as she led the way down a staircase. 'Ladies are not allowed in the audience, *naturellement*.'

The staircase was clean, but bare and there was no sign of opulence until Amanda was led through a door at the bottom. Here, what had once been perhaps four large cellars of the houses above had undergone conversion into a luxurious mini-theatre. There were a dozen rows of plush seats, tiered so that an audience of one hundred and twenty had an unobstructed view of what was obviously a stage behind the velvet curtains which concealed one end of the theatre.

The seats and curtains were scarlet and the walls and carpeting pure white.

'Take off your shoes, *s'il vous plaît,*' the girl requested, kicking free her own stiletto heeled footwear and accepting Amanda's.

Three men and a girl sat in a central position of the first row of seats and they all looked round expectantly as Amanda was led down the aisle at one side. She recognised Murville: tall, slim, effeminately good looking and slightly ridiculous in trendy clothes styled for a man at least half his forty years. She did not know the smartly-dressed, ugly man with greasy hair; the pretty young girl with a swollen jaw; or the fat teenage boy with acne and a nervous tic in his right cheek.

Nobody stood up as Amanda was halted in front of the first row of seats. Murville inclined his head in a token greeting. Calbiac raked her from head to foot with an insolent expression in his deep-set eyes. Jennifer Darwin had cried a lot on the trip from Chartres and was still in excruciating pain from the broken bone in her jaw. Her moist eyes poured scorn and hate on Amanda. The boy, a German named Werner Heck, licked his lips in obscene anticipation and fingered himself busily through his bulging jeans.

'Good even –' Amanda started.

'Sexy face,' Calbiac said in French, eyeing her now as if she were a piece of meat in a butcher's window. 'Pretty skinny. Is she small?'

Murville fitted a cheroot in a long ebony holder. 'That I don't know, Henri,' he replied. 'But the body looks good without clothes.' He lit the cheroot and the aroma of the smoke threatened to raise nausea in Amanda's throat. 'And if we shaved off her hair the contrast with Jacques would be magnificent.'

Jennifer made a small, plaintive sound and when Amanda looked at her she saw the young girl's expression undergo rapid changes: from contempt to horror and then sympathy. The spotty-faced boy began to finger his zipper and the tic suddenly took control of the entire side of his face. His bad breath cut through the acrid smoke of Murville's cheroot.

'We will examine her, Nana,' Calbiac instructed.

Amanda felt as she had at the café on the Champs Élysées. The girl with the big breasts gripped her upper arm and urged her towards a short flight of steps at the side of the theatre. There was a soft hum and the velvet curtains swished open. The bulbs in the wall fixtures dimmed and then a harsh white spotlight stabbed a finger from the rear of the theatre. It was impossible that this could be happening to her. It had to be a dream. She was the daughter of one of the richest men in the world and had the protection of the hardest and meanest man she had ever met. So how could she be in such a situation, unless as a part of some twisted nightmare?

But it had to be happening, of course. For as she stood in the centre of the stage, the spotlight hit her full in the face. Had she been dreaming, such intense brightness would surely wake her.

'You will take off your clothes so that Mr. Calbiac may see the lack of bodily hair.'

It was Murville talking to her, his soft tones floating up from the wide pool of darkness beyond the circle of light.

'But, I –'

'Nana!' Calbiac barked the name.

She thought the girl had left her, but then felt hot breath on the back of her neck as Nana leaned close.

'Do as he says,' she whispered. 'If you resist, I will hold you while Werner tears the clothes from you. Some girls enjoy that?' The final words had the intonation of a question.

Amanda felt hot, then cold. She kept repeating the name Stark to herself, but stopped afraid she might blurt it aloud. She crossed her arms in front of her, hooked her fingers around the ribbed hem of the sweater and jerked it over her head. Nana plucked it from her hands. She wore a black half bra underneath. Her fingers trembled and she could not unfasten the clasp. Nana knocked the quivering hands away and snapped open the fastening, pulling the flimsy garment free of Amanda's body. The small, brown-crested breasts thrust forward, creamy white against the even tan of her torso.

Amanda could hear Heck panting and thought she picked up the rip of a zipper a moment before she pulled down the one at the side of her leather skirt.

'I have seen men with bigger boobs than that!' Calbiac said with contempt.

'Wait, Henri,' Murville urged.

Amanda thought she was going to faint. She tried to reawaken the impression of a dream, but her mind refused to accept it. Sordid reality pressed in around her and sheened her body with shiny beads of perspiration as she allowed the skirt to fall around her ankles. *Christ,* she thought, *where is Stark*?

She hooked a thumb under the waistband of the black panties at each hip and jerked them down her trembling thighs, swiftly removing them and the tights at the same time.

Heck gasped and gave a short, high-pitched giggle.

'Lots of girls shave down there,' Calbiac said, unimpressed.

As Nana stooped to gather up the last of the discarded clothes, Amanda stood erect, legs slightly parted, arms hung loosely at her sides. The stance lacked the least spark of vitality. Her normally sensual face seemed somehow pathetically childlike in the abject misery of her expression. As Nana moved away, carrying the clothes, it seemed to emphasise her nakedness. The men's eyes staring up at her from out of the dark felt like dirty fingers probing the secret places of her sweat-drenched body.

'I know,' Murville said excitedly. 'But I never thought of it before. We can shave her head and the contrast will be complete.'

'Open your legs wider!' Calbiac ordered.

Amanda obeyed as a reflex action. She had reached the nadir of humiliation. There was no point in fighting because everything was lost. She had crossed the thin dividing line between love and hate. Stark had made her do this thing and so he was no better than the perverts who rasped instructions at her. As she turned, bent over, raised her arms and fondled herself, her repugnance for Stark reached the same degree of bitterness she felt for the men watching the obscene display.

'She looks small,' Calbiac announced and there was a hint of pleasure in his voice now. 'Perhaps there will be blood the first few times. The admission charge should be higher.'

'Every time!' Murville squealed. 'We can fake it when it doesn't happen any more.'

'Good, Maurice,' Calbiac congratulated. 'I like that. She will perform tonight.'

'That should be most amusing, Henri,' a new voice said.

Amanda realised it was a new voice and that it came from the rear of the theatre. But from the depths of her wretchedness, she could hear but not care. One further pair of male eyes exploring the secret places of her body made no difference.

'Who's there?' Murville demanded. 'Lights.'

The wall lights pricked the darkness and rapidly brightened. The spotlight continued to hold Amanda a prisoner on the centre of the stage with its garish backdrop of a jungle scene.

'François Flaud,' the newcomer announced, rising from a seat at the end of the rear row and starting down the aisle.

Enrico Primo's contact man at Nice was medium in all things – height, build and features. He was even middle aged. Tanned and emanating good health and self-assurance, he swaggered towards the front of the theatre with his very white dentures flashing in a smile. Calbiac stood up, grinning with an expression of genuine warmth as he extended his hand. Murville looked deferential. Jennifer gazed at Amanda in deep sorrow. Werner Heck zipped his jeans and slunk away through a door at the side of the stage.

'You like Maurice's new acquisition, eh?' Calbiac asked, pumping Flaud's hand. 'It is planned to team her with Jacques. The black girl has lost her novelty.'

Amanda met Flaud's smiling eyes and saw something behind them which struck fear into her heart.

'I like her,' Flaud replied. 'She's both rich and beautiful – a combination I find hard to resist in a woman.'

Although speaking to Calbiac, he continued to hold Amanda's nervous gaze. The top man in the French company swung his ugly face towards the nude girl on the stage. His expression became a cloud of confusion.

'Rich, François?'

'As all hell,' Flaud replied. 'She's turned her back on her father's fortune, but Stark is pretty well heeled with company money, Henri.'

Flaud dropped the smile now and his eyes became as hard as those of Calbiac. Even the weak handsomeness of Murville was twisted by a harsh menace as he stared at Amanda. For long moments she seemed to be turned to stone in the heavy silence that had descended over the theatre at the mention of Stark's name. Then she gave a low groan and whirled around. Fear was a physical weight in her stomach, but her muscles drew strength from panic. She lunged to the side of the stage. Even as she ran, she knew it was hopeless – that she could not escape from the trap into which Stark had made her walk. But at the edge of her panic there was a flicker of reason. It offered a hope in the broiling sea of hopelessness. One of the men might be shocked into an abrupt, thoughtless action. She prayed for the sound of a shot, the impact of a bullet ripping into her naked flesh: bringing death to protect her from the evil these men would direct towards her because they didn't have Stark.

Nana stepped out of the darkness at the side of the stage and raised a hand. But it held no gun. Amanda screamed and started to swerve away. But there was no time. The girl's hand folded into a fist and swung. The blow smacked into Amanda's throat. She gagged. The spotlight raked across the stage and for a split second seemed to hold her in suspended animation. Then unconsciousness drained support from her and she crumpled to the boards.

'How do you know?' Calbiac demanded, sweeping his gaze around to capture Flaud's attention.

'It's the reason I came to Paris, Henri,' Flaud said, very businesslike now as he reached into the inside pocket of his lightweight sports jacket. He pulled out a wallet and from it extracted a photograph. He handed it to Calbiac, who snatched it greedily. 'My man in Toulouse borrowed the original from a police contact. We had a section of the picture enlarged.'

Calbiac's eyes gorged on the photograph as if they felt a hunger it could satisfy. The sides of the picture were dark and blurred, unrecognisable as the shoulders of René and André Léger. The face framed by the car window in the background was also fuzzy from the enlarging process, but the features were definitely those of the girl curled up on the stage.

'Where?' Calbiac demanded, waving the photograph as if it were still wet from developing.

'The camera was found this morning,' Flaud replied. 'On a road some kilometers from where René, André and Saïd were killed. That is part of the last picture taken. It shows René and André with a car passing behind them. It seemed obvious the camera was thrown away in haste. I made a guess about who was in the car.' He shrugged, then flashed a brand new smile like a toothpaste advertisement. 'I had no idea it would be so easy to find the girl.'

Calbiac cracked open his wide mouth in a smile of his own. It had a touch of evil as he stared at the unconscious Amanda. 'And now we have her, it will be just as easy to find Stark,' he said softly, tapping the photograph against his teeth.

'You don't think it was coincidence, the girl being here?' Flaud asked.

'I allow coincidence to be stretched just so far,' the company's top man answered and swung towards the confused Murville. 'Maurice, call Fouchet. I want six cars covering the streets outside, in position in thirty minutes time. At least two men in a car. They will watch carefully when I leave with Stark's whore. But they will not apprehend him until we are clear of the city. Dead or alive, it is of no importance.'

Murville hurried to comply with the order, using a telephone in a wall shell at the rear of the theatre. Calbiac told Nana to rouse Amanda and this was done – with a bucket of cold water hurled over the naked flesh.

'Dress her!'

Amanda gasped her way into awareness, getting instant and total recall of what had happened up to the moment Nana hit her. In the grip of despair, she neither helped nor resisted as the well-endowed French girl dressed her dripping body.

'Where is Stark?' Calbiac barked at her.

'Who's Stark?' Amanda replied, the words raising pain

in her bruised throat. She was surprised at the response; wondered why she felt the need to defend Stark.

'Nana? Hurt, but awake.'

The French girl was standing behind Amanda, fastening the skirt zipper. Amanda's upper body was still nude. Nana's hands reached around her torso and clawed over the white firmness of Amanda's breasts. Amanda screamed as the strong fingers dug into her flesh.

'I don't know!' she shrieked. 'Outside somewhere. He said he'd be close by.'

Calbiac nodded and Nana released her two-handed grip. She continued to dress the captive girl, her fingers suddenly gentle.

'Fouchet will get right on to it, Henri,' Murville reported.

Calbiac dropped back into the seat. 'Good. You had better prepare for the show, Maurice.'

The tall homosexual nodded, eyeing Amanda's wretchedness with regret. 'So the finale will still be the black girl with Jacques?'

Calbiac shook his head and turned slowly to look at Jennifer. The girl gave a strangled sob and cowered away from him. 'No, Maurice. I like your idea. Bare skin contrasting with hair. It will not take long to shave this one – everywhere!'

'No, Henri!' Jennifer shrieked.

Now it was Amanda's turn to look at the girl with compassion – although she did not know the fate which awaited Jennifer.

Murville grinned broadly. 'Werner!' he yelled.

The German boy appeared at the doorway as Nana forced Amanda down the steps.

'Please, Henri!' Jennifer pleaded, the pain raging in her broken jaw as her lips wrenched wide to scream for mercy. 'Not Jacques! Anything but Jacques!'

'Keep her quiet and still,' Calbiac ordered, pointing at Amanda.

Nana nodded and thrust the fully dressed Amanda into a seat. She stood over her, hands on hips and enormous breasts thrusting forward in an attitude of menace. Calbiac swung around to indicate that the German should take Jennifer.

'Remove every hair from her body, Werner,' he instructed. Then he softened his tone to one of mock tenderness as he looked at the terrified girl. 'It's all right, my sweetness,' he said in English. 'You have no whiskers, so he will not need to touch your poor chin.'

As Heck reached towards the young girl, her eyes rolled up and snapped closed. Her body went limp into a dead faint of terror and she slid from the seat, the hem of her dress slipping up to reveal her transparent briefs. The display thrust Heck into greater haste and he lifted her inert body with ease and carried her through the doorway to backstage.

'I will go to prepare for the show,' Murville announced happily, prancing through the door and closing it behind him.

'What's so bad about this Jacques guy?' Flaud asked, dropping into a seat beside Calbiac and lighting a half-smoked Havana cigar.

An obscene grin added to Calbiac's ugliness. 'Heck brought him from Hamburg,' he replied. 'He's the club's biggest attraction – and I mean biggest, François!' A burst of laughter gusted from the wide mouth. 'A real hairy guy.'

'You mean . . .?' Flaud began.

'Almost human,' Calbiac replied, more laughter ripping from his slack mouth.

But the strain of having to force the mirth was showing now. It was all done with the mouth and shoulders. The deep-set eyes were wallowing on a sea of liquid fear that plumbed the depths to the man's stomach. Stark had come to Paris, where he could have only one main target.

Amanda could not see Calbiac's expression, and would probably have been unable to penetrate it anyway. For she was too concerned with holding back the nausea that made her own insides feel liquid. Then she won the struggle, her swollen throat providing a barrier to the rising sickness. And pity for the girl in Heck's evil hands swamped her, negating the horror of escaping the same fate herself.

The worst was yet to come for the defenceless girl and Amanda begged silent forgiveness for including Stark in her hatred of her tormentors. She was glad that she had undergone such humiliation and suffering if it led to the downfall of those responsible for her anguish. No, not downfall – death. Blazing, flesh-tearing, blood-gushing death in the same way the men had died by the stream among the trees.

Come and get the bastards, Stark, she urged in prayer.

'On your feet, we're leaving,' Calbiac rasped as, far off, Jennifer Darwin began to scream.

CHAPTER TWENTY

Stark reached the Latin Quarter by an indirect route, stopping off at the Gare du Nord where he placed the briefcase in a luggage locker. In the taxi on the way to the railway station he thrust the Mauser in his jacket pocket and the bigger Luger into his waistband on the other side.

But despite the detour, he reached The Menagerie Club with enough time to check out the surrounding area before Amanda arrived. He even saw Calbiac and Jennifer Darwin go through the unmarked doorway, without realising the identity of the stocky Frenchman. Flaud, who was also unknown to Stark, was admitted to the club about thirty minutes after Amanda went in.

Stark watched from a vantage point on the roof of the building above the cellar theatre. It was not a position that made him happy, but the best available in the circumstances. For it gave an unobstructed view of the street in front of the club: and a careless cat knocking over a bottle had proved he could hear any but the slightest noises from the littered cobbled courtyard at the back.

His misgivings concerned the fact that there was no entrance into the building from the roof and there was certainly no way of seeing what was happening inside. He reached the roof by climbing on to an outbuilding and then shinning up a drainpipe at the rear. The windows he had passed on the way were uncurtained but he was unable to penctrate the darkness on the other side. Window-ledges piled with paper, ink bottles, books and other stationery items suggested it was an office building. The whole place was as silent as it was dark.

Stretched out full-length down the shallow incline of the tiles, periodically peering over the moss-choked gutter to look into the street, he sweated much more than the spring warmth of the night demanded. He cursed the need to use somebody else in his fight against the company. Then he changed the wide-ranging *somebody* to Amanda, and his failure to provide an escape route as she had asked, sharpened his bitterness.

But a moment later a fresh sound against the low background hum of the city interrupted his thoughts and he inched forward to peer down into the street. A few cars had swept by and two had parked, their occupants climbing out and clattering back to the boulevard. He had taken note of them, but dismissed them as innocent incidents with no threat of danger. But the convoy of six cars which now swung into the street carried a sinister undertone. The six pairs of yellow headlights were like alert eyes raking the street and the rumble of the engines seemed to hold a note of evil eagerness.

The leading car stopped and reversed into an alleyway. Two angled to one side of the street and two to the other and parked. The final car went to the far end of the street, made a U-turn and stopped, facing the way it had come. Lights and engines were switched off. Paris hummed, a quiver of sound in the warm night air.

The sweat pumped from Stark's pores as he waited for the cars to spill out their occupants. Doors stayed firmly closed. The sweat froze. For long seconds, he felt paralysed, his mind working at a frenetic pace: racing to discover how the company had known about Amanda – refusing to conceive the thousand and one horrific ways they might have made her talk.

Then he was inching up to the peak of the roof and making faster progress down the other side. The drainpipe creaked under his weight and the cat scampered away, rolling the bottle again. He had to climb a wall at the rear of the courtyard to reach a rubbish littered alleyway which intersected the wider one into which the car had reversed. When he reached the meeting point, he jerked the Luger from his waistband before peering around the angle of crumbling brickwork. The rear elevation of the parked car showed as a silhouette against the pale glow of street lights. Through the window he could see the shadowy forms of two men seated in the front seats. The high walls of the buildings on either side trapped a pregnant silence between them. As Stark flattened himself against one of the walls and moved forward, he could hear the tick of the car's engine cooling.

The men had both front windows rolled down and Stark could hear a low rumble of whispered conversation. The flow of French was too fast for Stark to understand it. He crouched down beside the rear off-side wheel and wondered how to silence the men without making a noise in the process.

Footfalls sounded out in the street.

'Get ready,' one of the men said in his native tongue.

'Okay,' the driver answered.

The footsteps were crossing the street and Stark was sure he recognised the sound of two men and a woman. A car door opened and, a few moments later, slammed shut. A single pair of footfalls and then another door. A starter motor whirred and the engine caught. The car beside Stark roared into raucous life, filling his nostrils with acrid exhaust fumes. He went forward, straightening. The surprised face of a man stared out at him. He thrust the Luger in through the window and felt the impact of the muzzle against flesh. He squeezed the trigger.

There was hardly any recoil. The man did not utter a dying sound. Blood from the hole in his temple spurted over the gun and Stark's right hand. Stark jerked open the door and the body toppled out from behind the wheel. The man in the passenger seat struggled to reach for something under his jacket. Stark squeezed the Luger's trigger again. The bullet ripped into the man's armpit and burrowed down into his heart. He slumped forward with a gasp.

A black Cadillac convertible with the top up swept by the end of the alley and Stark recognised it as the car in which the stocky man and the brunette had arrived. The engine of the Renault into which Stark slid was still running. Out on the street several other engines were masking the throb of the city's heartbeat.

He closed the door and wrestled the dead weight of his passenger into a sitting position and held him there by fastening the seat belt. The car which had made the U-turn crawled past the mouth of the alley, the driver gesturing a signal with a raised hand. Stark was grateful the car was yet another Renault R8. He did not have to fumble for the light switch. The heads splashed on at full beam, hiding the body in the alley behind their dazzle. He shot the car forward, into a screaming turn on to the street. The body of the dead man in the front passenger seat rocked, but was held upright by the safety harness.

The big Cadillac swung into a right turn on to Boulevard St. Germain and the R16 ahead of Stark swung out to overtake. Stark moved up closer to the limousine. Behind him the other four cars which had been parked in the area of the club formed a convoy.

The driver of the car which had slotted into the leading position took a zig-zagging course through the south-western arrondissements of the city, holding his speed to the maximum or below. All the cars behind Stark stayed on station.

To Stark, it seemed like a stupid method of flushing him into the open – if, indeed, that was the object of the exercise. But he made allowances for a hurried decision. Amanda had been spotted for what she was and somebody had to think of something fast. By the same token, he himself had been required to institute a rapid counterplan without time to consider all the eventualities. Jesus, he thought as the convoy picked up speed on a dual carriageway section of the N10 west of Versailles, he couldn't even be sure the girl in the Cadillac was Amanda.

He tried to tell himself it didn't matter – that the big limousine was as much a status symbol in the company as any other strata of society: ergo its male occupants were big-time targets worthy of his lethal attention. So, even if the Cadillac did not contain the top man himself, those travelling in its high-priced comfort would be in a position to point the finger.

His mind would not accept the premise. Amanda had become as much a part of him as his hate-filled ambition to smash the company. It angered him to have to admit it, but he was forced to accede to the fact. Something – someone – had been elevated to a higher priority than the vendetta.

The foolishness of the company plan played into Stark's hands. There was no interchanging of positions as the convoy sped through the forests around Rambouillet and stayed on the N10 road across the seemingly endless plain of Beauce. Traffic was light in both directions as today was relegated to yesterday: night becoming a new morning with a slight breeze to chill the warmth out of the air. Occasionally, a strange car swung out and leap-frogged along the line of the company convoy. Stark guessed that this relieved the boredom and set pulses racing. But always the intruder would roar on ahead along the black ribbon of road between the vast fields of sprouting wheat.

Stark's pulse maintained a high rate for the entire trip. Anxiety for Amanda gnawed at one part of his mind while another was in a turmoil over the danger of his position. The dead man at his side, head lolling forward on his chest, was a constant and vivid warning of what could happen to Stark: and a reminder of what might already have happened to Amanda.

He drove with the window rolled halfway down to keep the car's interior free of the smell of death. But he didn't notice the drop in temperature brought by the early hours of a new day: the sweat of fear insulated him from the weather.

Grim and dusty, locked-up-for-the-night farming villages flashed past, the dark walls of the buildings resounding with the subdued rumble of car engines. Then the lights of Chartres threw up an orange dome against the monotonous horizon, like some ethereal emanation from the city's great cathedral, standing out starkly from the sea of cornfields.

The leading car made a right turn on to a narrow side road. The Cadillac followed and Stark led the way for the remainder of the convoy. The road ran arrow straight between a twin row of poplars. Its surface was uneven and scattered with potholes. The Renault juddered and pitched. Stark cursed and drove with one hand on the wheel, his other pressed against the shoulder of the dead man to keep him upright. The headlights of the car behind him held the Renault in a wavering splash of yellow brilliance. Stark knew that he and his inert passenger would show up as a pair of dark silhouettes to the men in the car behind.

The countryside ahead offered no relief to monotony except for Calbiac's château, standing five hundred metres back from the road at the end of a tarmac drive flanked by more poplars. The boundary of the property was marked by white-painted fencing through which the artificial lake behind the house glinted with reflected moonlight.

Brake lights glowed and the seven cars closed up as the turn was made. The house, ugly and rambling, had a grim, forbidding appearance in the harshness of the headlights. The driveway opened out into a wide area of paved apron at the front of the house. There was a lazily spouting fountain at the centre and shade trees at the sides.

Stark released his grip on the dead man and pulled the Luger from his waistband as the Cadillac whispered to a halt at the foot of a wide set of steps narrowing up to the front door of the château. The leading car angled to a halt at the right hand side of the paved apron. Stark slowed the Renault to a crawl as he swung to the opposite side of the central fountain, his eyes narrowing to glittering slits as he watched the Cadillac.

All the other cars swerved to the right and parked in echelon. The stocky man with the greased-down hair climbed out of the driver's door of the limousine. His ugly face was florid with anger. He jerked open the rear door and reached inside. Stark's grip tightened on the butt of the Luger as he saw Amanda stagger out of the car. The man shoved her forward and she gasped, tripping and falling up the steps. The Renault went around the corner of the house and Stark could see no more.

CHAPTER TWENTY-ONE

'A goddamn washout!' Calbiac raged, his hand arcing towards the frightened face of Jean Fouchet. The palm caught the trembling flesh of the cheek with a sharp smacking sound and the victim staggered to the side, biting back a groan of pain.

The drawing room of the château was spacious enough not to look crowded. Amanda was sitting back in a big winged chair to one side of an impressive fireplace. Flaud did not have to touch her to hold her prisoner in the chair. The grimness of his tanned face was sufficient to keep the girl cowed. He was the only occupant of the room to show any interest in her. The centre of attention was the raging Calbiac, who stood over the stooped and quaking form of Fouchet in an attitude indicating he was about to launch a further physical attack against the man.

But he didn't. Instead, he fixed the terrified Fouchet with a penetrating stare and lashed him with his tongue.

'You are an imbecile!' he roared, splashing spittle on to the other's face. 'You are incapable of doing anything more than torturing a defenceless man – providing that man is held by another. You do not have the brains of a two-year-old child. Did you really expect somebody so cunning as this Englishman to fall into a trap when you did everything short of making an announcement on television?'

Calbiac continued to rant at the luckless head of the company's Paris enforcers, the diatribe becoming laced with profanity as the ugly director of Drake et Cie. underlined the many flaws in Fouchet's method.

'But there was not time to . . .' Fouchet began at one point, but allowed his plaintive voice to trail away as Calbiac's eyes bored into his own.

Fouchet was taller, stronger and younger than Calbiac. The nine others who looked on were cast from similar moulds, their lack of brain power compensated for by an obvious hardness apparent in their thick-set bodies. But respect out of fear for the company's top man negated their strength. They stood around in an embarrassed silence, grateful that Fouchet's responsibility for the abortive plan acted as a buffer between themselves and Calbiac's fury.

Finally, the ugly man ran out of epithets and he swung away from his victim, his bright eyes stabbing a hateful stare at Amanda.

'But we still have the bastard's whore!' he exclaimed, the force of his words driving Amanda hard back against the chair. But as Flaud stepped aside and Calbiac approached her, there was nowhere else to go. He reached out a pudgy hand and grasped a fistful of her auburn hair. He twisted it, jerking her head upright and bursting a cry of pain from her lips. The bruise on her throat was yellow against the tanned skin. 'If he cares about anything in this world, he cares about her,' Calbiac continued, turning around to face his audience, forcing Amanda on display again.

Ten pairs of pitiless eyes fastened on to her face in unwavering stares.

'She is no raving beauty,' Calbiac continued, 'but Stark must find her appealing.' His eyes locked on Fouchet's face, then swung around to take in the other men in a glower of anger. 'You will all return to Paris and circulate word that we have the girl. Unless Stark surrenders himself to us within three days, his whore will die. And she will not die easily.'

He emphasised his point. His own strength became apparent as he raised his clenched fist. Amanda screamed as she was lifted bodily from the chair by her hair. When he thudded her back into it, he did not relinquish his grip.

Stark was at the head of the sweeping stairway when he heard the girl's cry of agony. Getting into the house had been easy. He left the car at the side and reached the rear in a loping run. The water of the lake rippled and gurgled as the cool breeze skated over it. The same breeze dried the sweat on his face. He was just passing the french windows of the drawing room when a wedge of light splashed through them. As he lunged into the darkness on the other side, he caught a glimpse of Amanda as she was thrust violently into the room and went sprawling to the rich carpet.

'Stay with it, darling,' he muttered, feeling the adrenalin begin to pump through him as he sensed his plan had worked. For the ugly man had the air of authority and the luxurious trappings of a very big wheel indeed – perhaps even the biggest. But if he wasn't the number one man in the French company, he would do. For it was he who was giving Amanda the treatment and in Stark's new order of priorities, that marked him down for death.

Between the rear wall of the château and the edge of the lake there was a flag-stone patio. He crossed this silently, to where a modern, brick-built extension to the house projected several feet out into the moon-silvered water. There was a wooden walkway alongside the new section of the building and he moved out on to it. At the end, it broadened into a jetty. Water lapped into the extension through the open end. Out of reach of the breeze, the surface was smooth and the power boat and two dinghies moored inside rode at an immobile rest.

There was a wider walkway inside the boathouse and Stark went stealthily along it to the concrete area at the darkened rear. The place smelled of tar and diesel oil. He paused for a few moments, allowing his eyes to grow accustomed to the darkness. Against one wall was a workbench and above this a rack filled with a variety of tools. He selected a sheath knife and cut a length of cord from the reel. He put both cord and knife in his pocket and went up a flight of wooden steps to a door at the top. The handle turned and the door folded inwards with a slight squeak. It was pitch-black on the other side and he had to use his sense of touch to orientate himself in a small, bare hallway with a door at right angles to the one which had been unlocked. This one failed to open, but after a few seconds of probing with the knife blade, the lock tongue snapped back.

He cracked open the door and peered through. He looked down a long landing to a patch of suffused light at the far end. A voice reached him as a low rumble of fast, angry French. He opened the door wide, closed it behind him and took long strides towards the light source. He was at the head of an elegant banistered staircase which swept down into the centre of the two-storey hallway of the château. The hallway was lit by wall fixtures and a brighter wedge of light angled out from the open doorway of the drawing room. He thought the lights flickered when Amanda screamed, but in the next instant realised he had blinked.

'Sainteny is our man for that, M. Calbiac,' Fouchet said

nervously. 'His café is the ideal place to feed the grapevine.'

'I don't give a damn who puts out the word –'

'Where is Sainteny?' Fouchet said suddenly, interrupting the still angry voice of Calbiac.

'He was in Alain's car,' somebody said.

'Alain drove to the side of the house,' another of the men supplied.

'Keep talking,' Stark muttered to himself, flattening his body against the wall and moving back along the landing to a point where he could see the doorway of the drawing room and yet duck back out of sight in a split-second.

'Jesus Christ Almighty!' Flaud shouted. 'Henri, do you –'

'Go and check the car!' Calbiac screamed, an edge of fear adding a tremor to his voice.

Stark drew the Luger and his sweat glands began to work overtime again. Fouchet lumbered out into the hallway, a gun in his fist, fear in his eyes. He ran to the front door, jerked it open and dashed outside. His footfalls were loud on the paved apron in front of the château. Stark smelled French cigarette smoke and it reminded him how much he hated Paris – more than ever now. Running footsteps sounded again, faster this time and getting closer. Fouchet burst in through the front door.

'Sainteny's dead!' he shouted, his face grey, his eyes wide with horror. 'Alain has gone.'

He started to go back into the drawing room, but Calbiac's furious voice halted him. 'Search the house and grounds! Move, you stupid bastards. François, you too. I'll keep the girl here.'

Stark understood *recherche, maison* and *jardin*. Also, *fille*. He saw Fouchet turn and dash back towards the front door as a half dozen men ran from the room, all armed. Four took off in pursuit of Fouchet and two headed for the foot of the stairway. The remainder of the men streamed out into the hallway, but Stark did not see them. He backed along the landing and pushed open a door. Moonlight filtered through lace curtains to show up bedroom furniture. He left the door ajar and stood behind it, holding his breath. He recognised the sound of more than two men on the carpeted stairs.

Only one came into the room as the door folded open

wide. He held the revolver extended in front of him. He looked at the wrong side of the room first and when he started to turn, it was too late. The knife was already thrusting towards him with all Stark's weight behind it. The sharp point burst through the tight skin of the man's throat and plunged deep. He died with a low gurgle of arterial blood. Stark withdrew the knife and caught the body before it could thud to the floor. He dragged it behind the door and lowered it softly. The gun was still held by a death-tight fist.

Out on the landing, four men were shouting at each other as they banged open doors and peered fearfully into empty rooms. A shot exploded, fired at a shadow.

'You have him?' somebody yelled from downstairs.

'A mistake!' a voice replied.

'Imbeciles!' Calbiac screamed.

Stark moved into the doorway and poked out his head to look along the landing. One man was in sight, his back to him as he approached the door to the hallway above the boathouse. He discovered the traces of a forced entry and cursed. The three others lunged out of doorways and gathered around the first to examine the broken lock. Two of them turned to head back along the landing.

But Stark had stepped from cover and was bearing down upon them. They shouted and brought up their guns. The other two spun around. Stark went into a crouch and held out both arms in front of him. The Luger was in his right fist, the Mauser in the left. He pumped shells across a range of less than four metres and saw red patches blossom on the men's chests. Two of them got off shots as they fell. One bullet tugged at Stark's coat sleeve. Another gouged a rut in the ceiling and showered him with plaster dust.

'Un faux pas!' he yelled in response to a panicky inquiry from downstairs, aware that his accent would be detected – and that the dozen or more gunshots could not possibly be excused as a mistake.

He threw aside his empty guns and scooped up a Magnum and a Colt Automatic from amid the pile of blood-soaked bodies in the doorway. Then he stepped over them and into the dark of the hallway. There was shouting both inside and outside the house. And footfalls on the wooden stairway at the back of the boathouse. Somebody demanded silence, the roar cutting across every other sound. The noise ended abruptly. Except for a low creak to signal the approach of the man on the stairway. Then the squeak of the door cracking open.

Stark held his breath and sweated, a gun in each hand and the length of cord pulled tight between them. Fouchet was also holding his breath as he stepped into the darkness of the hallway. It was trapped inside his arching body, hot and foul, as Stark dropped the cord over the man's head and crossed his hands at the back of his neck. The guns clinked together and Fouchet's own revolver bounced off his shoe as Stark tightened the noose and thrust his knee into the small of the man's back. Flesh bulged around the taut cord. Fouchet struggled for long moments before he died. The trapped air sighed from his lungs as his body was lowered to the floor.

'Stark!'

The sound of his name, distant but loud, shouted by Calbiac with all the might he could muster, seemed to reverberate around the inside of Stark's skull like the pain from a blow. He froze in the act of straightening from placing Fouchet's body on the floor. He felt physically and mentally exhausted and knew the reason for this. He wanted to take out every company man in the world – but not all at once. And it was as if the whole stinking mass of them were surrounding him now. Figuring on two men from each car, including the Cadillac, that meant twelve had come to the château. He had killed six of them and in so doing had used up whatever element of surprise had been on his side – and all the luck he could count on. It had also drained him of the capacity to think and the strength to act.

Then he shook his head, to clear it of defeatist thoughts and as a gesture of his refusal to submit to them. So the odds were stacked against him? They had been that way from the moment he decided to embark upon his vendetta of hate. It wasn't this factor which probed slimy tentacles of doubt into his mind. His emotions had been thrown into a turmoil by anxiety for Amanda and it was this which had robbed him of the icy coolness that normally partnered the calmness of action whenever he killed.

'Stark? Can you hear me?' Calbiac's heavily accented English reached Stark as nothing more than a raised voice.

His brain was working smoothly now, disregarding extraneous concern for Amanda. She had lost her priority: had become merely another victim of the company's evil.

'I will kill the girl if you do not surrender, Stark!'

They had killed Carol. He had survived. Feeling – and moving – like a remote-controlled machine, Stark stepped over Fouchet's twisted body and went down the stairway, dropping the cord and knife into the dark water as he went along the inner walkway. He peered along the outside of the wall and in the moonlight the rear of the château with the flagged patio before it offered no hiding places. He went up on to the balls of his feet and reached the patio without making a sound. He crossed to the windows flanking the french doors of the drawing room. In the light, his face was like a grey plaster mask. It was completely expressionless. The eyes looked dead. But they were not. They registered the scene in the room and printed an image on a brain that accepted it stoically. The brain, with the dispassion of a programmed computer, issued an instruction. Muscles reacted in a split-second.

A leg was raised and the heel of Stark's shoe smashed at the centre of the double doors. They crashed open and he lunged into the room.

Calbiac was in the doorway of the hall, out of sight from the stairs. One of his hands was folded around Amanda's upper arm, fingers digging painfully into her flesh.

'I'm going to count ten and....'

He whirled around, terror quivering in every line and angle of his ugly face.

'Hit the floor!' Stark roared.

The girl was as scared as her captor. But the numbness of horror left her a moment before Calbiac achieved his recovery. As he jerked her in front of him, she was already falling. The guns in Stark's fist bucked, belching death across the big room. Amanda screamed and fell to the floor, released by Calbiac. The man staggered back through the doorway, a thick curtain of blood rolling down his dead face from two holes in his forehead. As the strength left his legs, he sat down and slumped backwards.

Amanda, screaming, scampered into cover as a fusillade of shots whined in through the doorway, splintering woodwork and snagging at the carpet.

He didn't hear her. The brain which had been programmed to destroy life could feel nothing that she had survived.

Another burst of gunfire exploded and a hail of bullets penetrated the drawing room. Stark was rooted to the spot, arms extended in front of him, the guns like two parts of him growing from his rock-steady hands.

Amanda stared at him, imploring him to instruct her. But he said nothing, and remained motionless. Suddenly she thrust to her feet and started to run, a third eruption of shots urging her to even greater speed.

'Come on!' she screamed as she flashed by him and out into the night.

More, the ice-cold brain demanded. *Kill every one of them.*

He took a step forward, hearing voices out in the hallway.

'Mort!' He knew what that meant.

He fired a shot out through the doorway to prove he was not dead. The bullet thudded into the waxen flesh of the dead Calbiac. The shot was answered by a fusillade. The company men were firing wildly, nobody in a position to aim. Stark felt untouchable as the bullets smashed harmlessly into walls, floor and furniture.

A powerful engine burst into life, but it was unconnected with the men out in the hallway. It could be disregarded. He took another step closer to the doorway and a bullet chipped a piece of leather from the sole of his left shoe.

'Stark!'

Amanda's voice. Behind him. The engine note had lowered to a gentle throb.

'Stark, please!'

A glance over his shoulder was allowed. The powerboat bobbed at the foot of the steps on the other side of the patio. It was sleek and red, gleaming in the light from the windows. Amanda looked frail and vulnerable as she stood on the seat behind the wheel. She held her arms out in front of her, beckoning him towards her with both hands.

A single shot sounded and the Colt was wrenched from his hand. His thumb spouted blood. He twisted his head around to stare at the doorway and now his face showed expression. The ice-coldness poured from his brain. It swept down to engulf his whole body. He wasn't a machine controlled by a computer. He was vulnerable flesh and blood, as easy to destroy as the objects of his hate.

The man who had shot at him was in view at one side of the doorway, lining up his gun for a second attempt.

'Stark!' The outboard of the powerboat gave a throaty roar. 'I'm going, for Christ's sake.'

Stark, weak with fear now, squeezed the trigger of the Magnum. The man in the doorway took the .357 bullet in the chest and reeled back. Blood arced from his shattered body as his scream was drowned by a burst of gunshots.

But Stark didn't see him. He pivoted and ran. The boat was pulling away from the steps and Amanda no longer looked frail as she crouched over the wheel. The patio seemed a mile across. Gunshots exploded behind him and the driving force of terror made up for weakness. Two bullets snagged his flapping jacket. He launched himself from the top of the steps and for an agonising moment was certain he had misjudged the dive.

Then Amanda glanced over her shoulder, her eyes and mouth wide with horror. She eased up on the throttle for a moment. Stark hit the water. His hands, one still holding the Magnum, clawed over the side of the boat.

'Go!' he screamed at her as a bullet ricocheted off the outboard cowling and another cracked the fibreglass hull.

The boat roared forward, its raked bow canting high out of the water. Stark's body adopted an almost horizontal posture as he was dragged across the lake. His arms felt as if they were being ripped from their sockets. Bullets reached for the boat, the sound of the guns masked by the roar of the engine. Within moments, they were out of range.

Amanda eased off the throttle and the boat settled its entire length into the water. She had to help him over the side and into the passenger seat. The gunshots sounded like distant fireworks. The bullets fell far short of the target.

The lake was big. It took a full five minutes to cross with the boat powered along at full speed. Stark said nothing, and neither did Amanda. They needed time and the privacy of their own thoughts to repair their shattered nerves.

A shingle beach appeared ahead of them and Amanda let up on the throttle too late.

'Hold on!' she yelled.

The flat keel smacked against dry land and skidded to a halt, gouging a deep rut across the shingle. The engine cut out and silence was absolute.

'Women drivers,' Stark muttered, and grinned at Amanda.

She started to laugh and it edged towards hysteria. Stark lashed out a hand and it smacked hard against her cheek. She stared at him, without rancour.

'You're absolutely, stark raving bloody mad,' she said softly.

'It's part of my fatal charm,' he replied. 'We're both in the same boat. Come on, darling. Let's get out of here.'

He helped her over the side and led her up the beach. His body was shaking and he told himself it was because of his wet clothes.

'*Qui est?*'

A gendarme moved out of the shadow of a tree. He wheeled a bicycle with one hand and pointed a revolver with the other.

'Shoot him!' Amanda shrieked, the sight of another gun threatening to push her into hysteria again.

Stark shook his head and lowered the Magnum he had levelled as a reflex action. 'Not a copper,' he said.

Amanda made a sound of disgust, then swung to face the gendarme again as he asked her about the noise at Calbiac's château.

'I was attacked,' Amanda said hurriedly in her fluent French. 'This man rescued me. Look what they did to me.' She changed to English. 'Get ready,' she hissed.

She crossed her arms in front of her body and curled her fingers under the hem of her sweater. She jerked up her hands, snagging the bra. Her breasts fell free of restraint, thrusting towards the startled gendarme, whose eyes swept away from Stark to drink in the sight of naked flesh.

Stark's right foot lunged towards the gendarme and sank into the man's groin. The uniformed figure struggled to swing his gun arm around, but the pain was too great and he folded forward, his bicycle crashing to the side. The Magnum barrel thudded into the exposed neck and the gendarme pitched to the ground, unconscious.

'Is this where my escape route ends?' Amanda asked,

covering herself with the sweater, watching him as he picked up the bicycle and swung on to the saddle.

'You have too many uses, darling,' he said, thrusting the Magnum into his pocket and beckoning for her to sit on the crossbar of the bicycle.

'Like almost getting killed for you?' she suggested, adopting the position he indicated.

'And keeping me abreast of unexpected developments,' he replied, starting to pedal away from the beach.